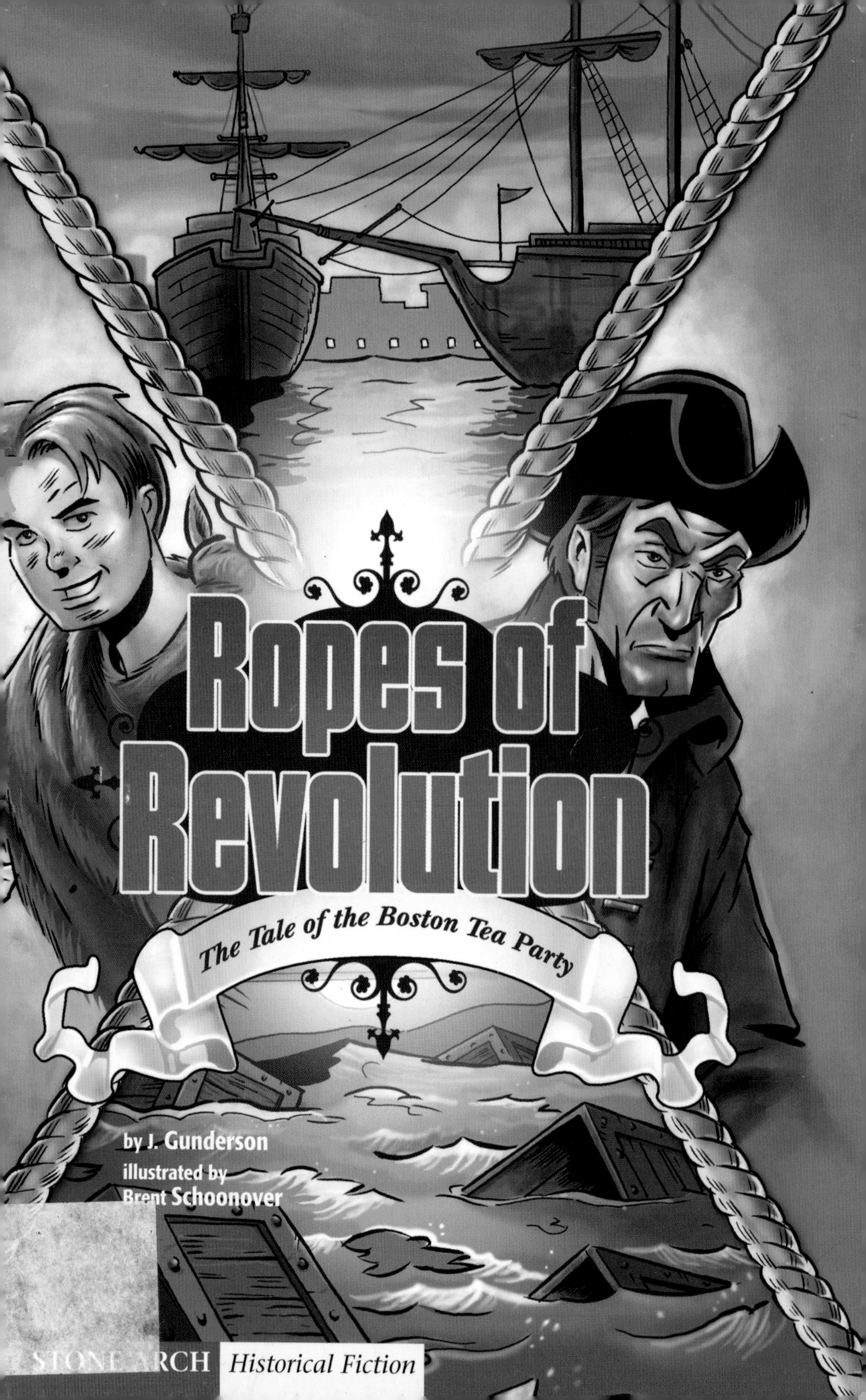
Ropes of Revolution
The Tale of the Boston Tea Party
by J. Gunderson
illustrated by
Brent Schoonover
STONE ARCH
Historical Fiction

TABLE OF CONTENTS

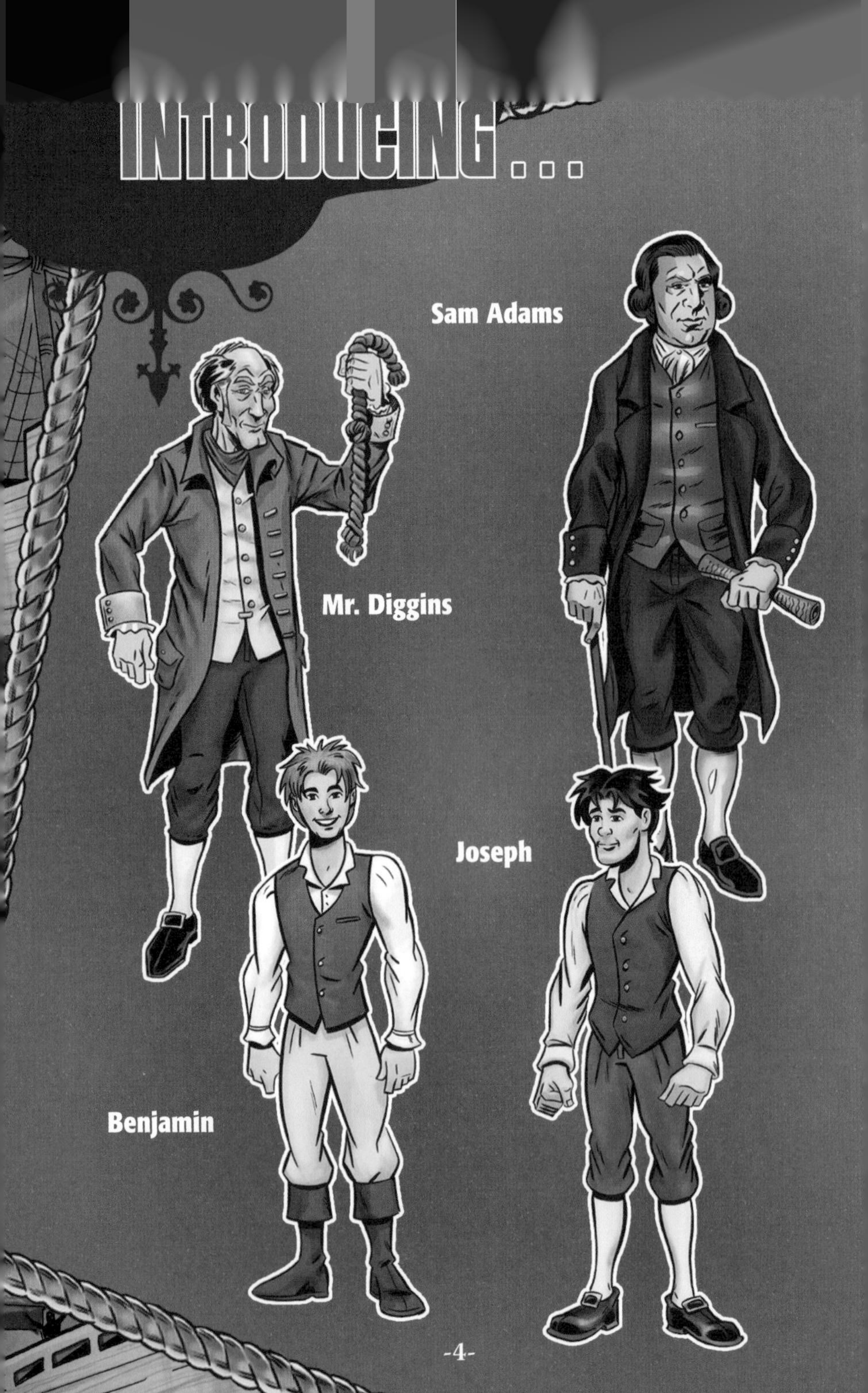
INTRODUCING...
Sam Adams
Mr. Diggins
Joseph
Benjamin

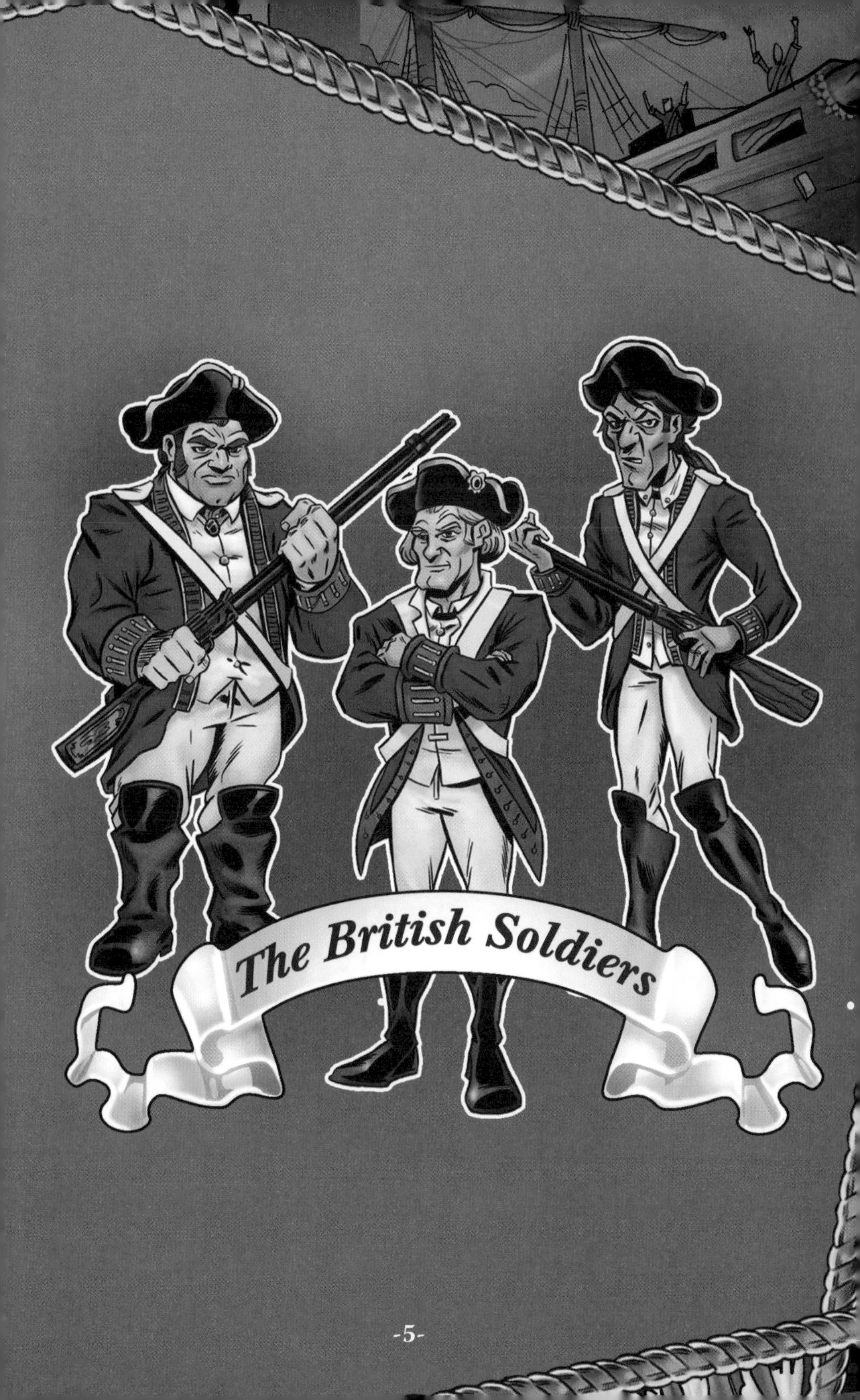
The British Soldiers

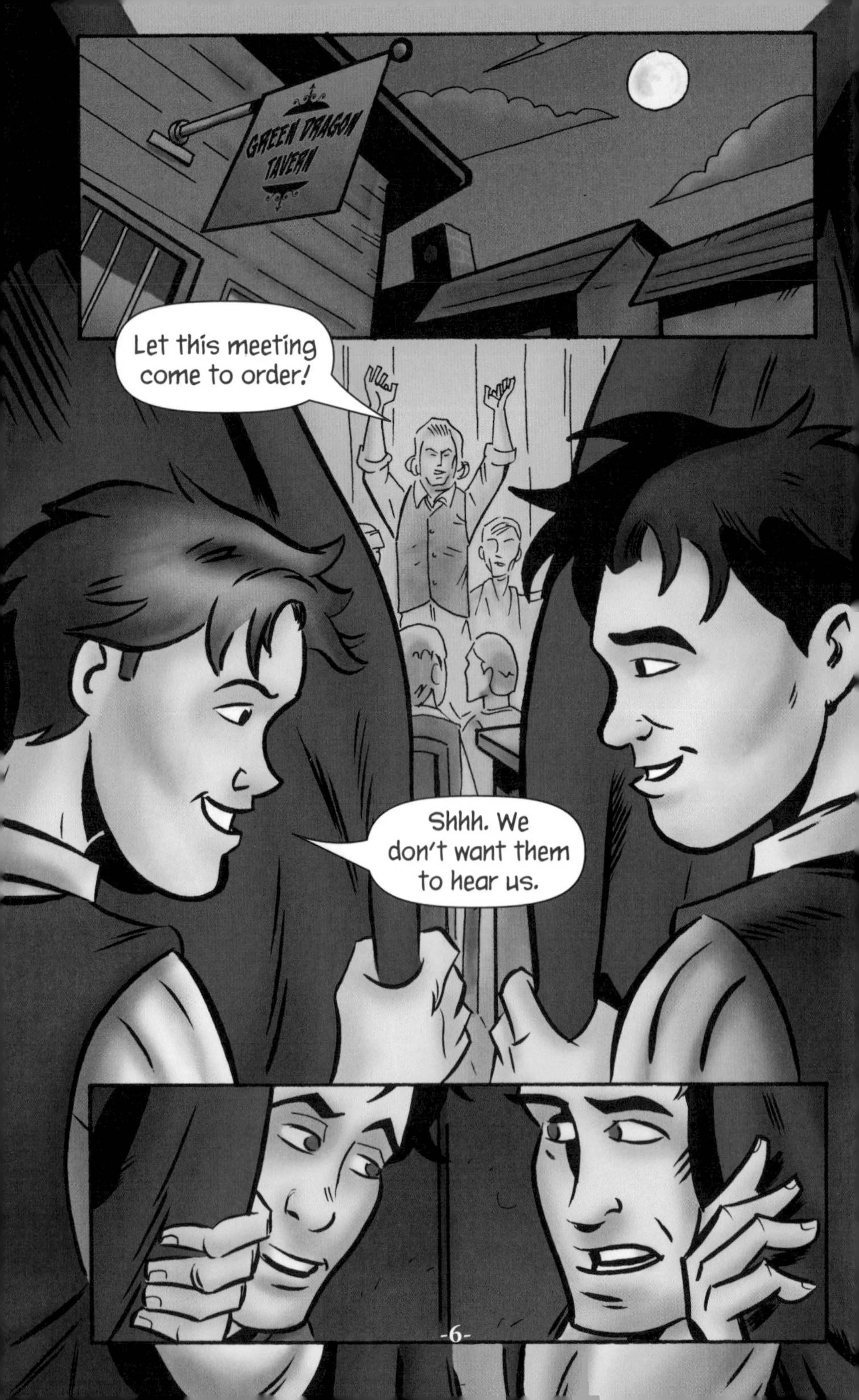
GREEN DRAGON TAVERN
Let this meeting come to order!
Shhh. We don't want them to hear us.

Chapter 1

THE SECRET MEETING

The walls of the Green Dragon Tavern shake with angry voices. From my hiding spot behind the cloak rack, I can see the voices belong to Samuel Adams, John Adams, and Paul Revere. These men are the Sons of Liberty.

I want to stand and shout with them. I know that my friend Joseph, standing right next to me, feels the same. But we are just young apprentices, only fifteen years old. Samuel Adams would never let us join the Sons of Liberty.

So Joseph and I are stuck here, on a December night in 1773, in the middle of a bunch of old cloaks.

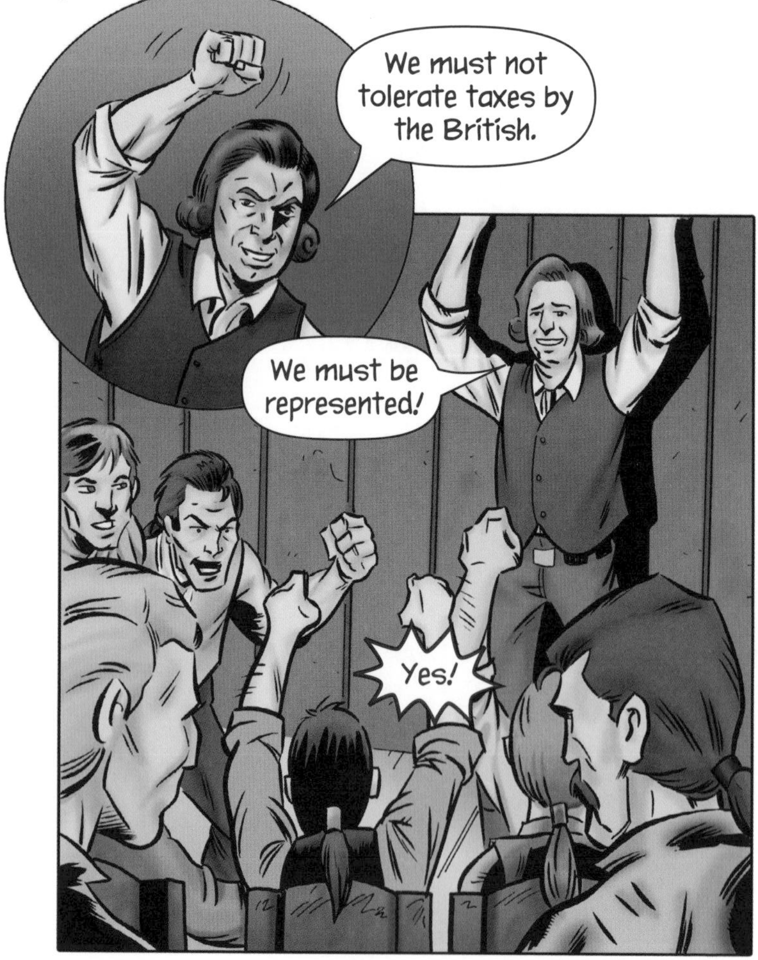
We must not tolerate taxes by the British.
We must be represented!
Yes!

I poke my head between the cloaks to hear better. The smell of coffee, ale, and gingerbread fills my nose.

Mr. Adams lowers his voice. “If Governor Hutchinson does not order the tea-bearing ships to leave Boston —”

"We'll take matters into our own hands!" I yell out from behind the rack.

Joseph grabs me by the neck and pulls me backward into the cloaks. "Benjamin! What are you doing?" he nearly shouts. "They'll catch us for sure!"

"Nobody saw me," I whisper.

"Let's get out of here," he says.

"All right," I agree. "We've heard what we needed to hear."

We creep out the door and into the night. A thin blanket of snow shines in the glow of the street lanterns. A British soldier, keeping watch at the corner, stares at us.

We talk about the secret meeting at the Green Dragon. The British have been raising taxes on the American colonies since 1763. Just last spring, the British ordered a new tax on tea. If that weren't bad enough, the British king sent soldiers to watch over us.

All of the colonists are boycotting tea. None of us will buy it. In New York, the colonists forced the ships with tea to leave without unloading. Here, in Boston, Governor Hutchinson said the tea must be unloaded by midnight on December 16, or we'll have to pay the whole tax.

December 16 is tomorrow. But I know that Samuel Adams and the other Sons of Liberty will never allow the tea to be unloaded. They have a plan.

If all goes well, the fishes in the harbor will soon be sipping English tea. Joseph and I want to help serve it.

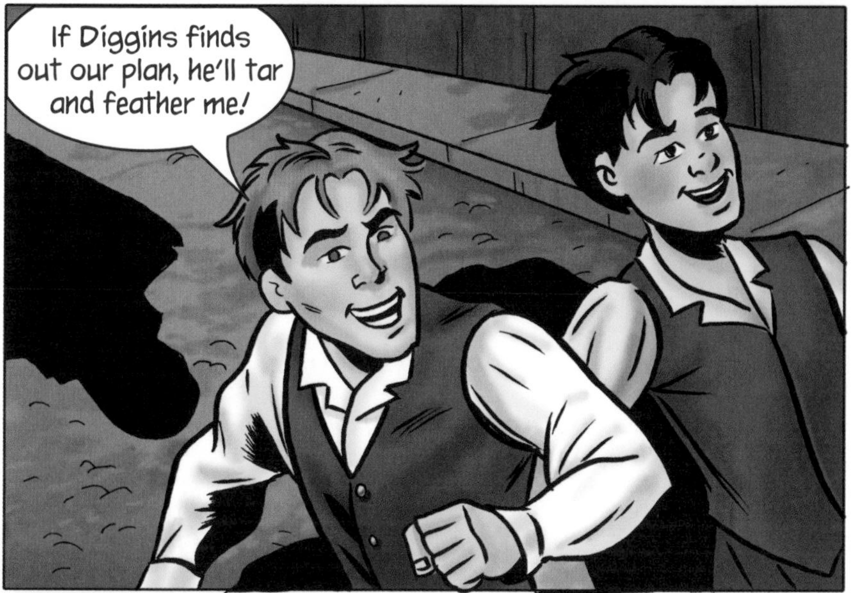
If Diggins finds out our plan, he'll tar and feather me!

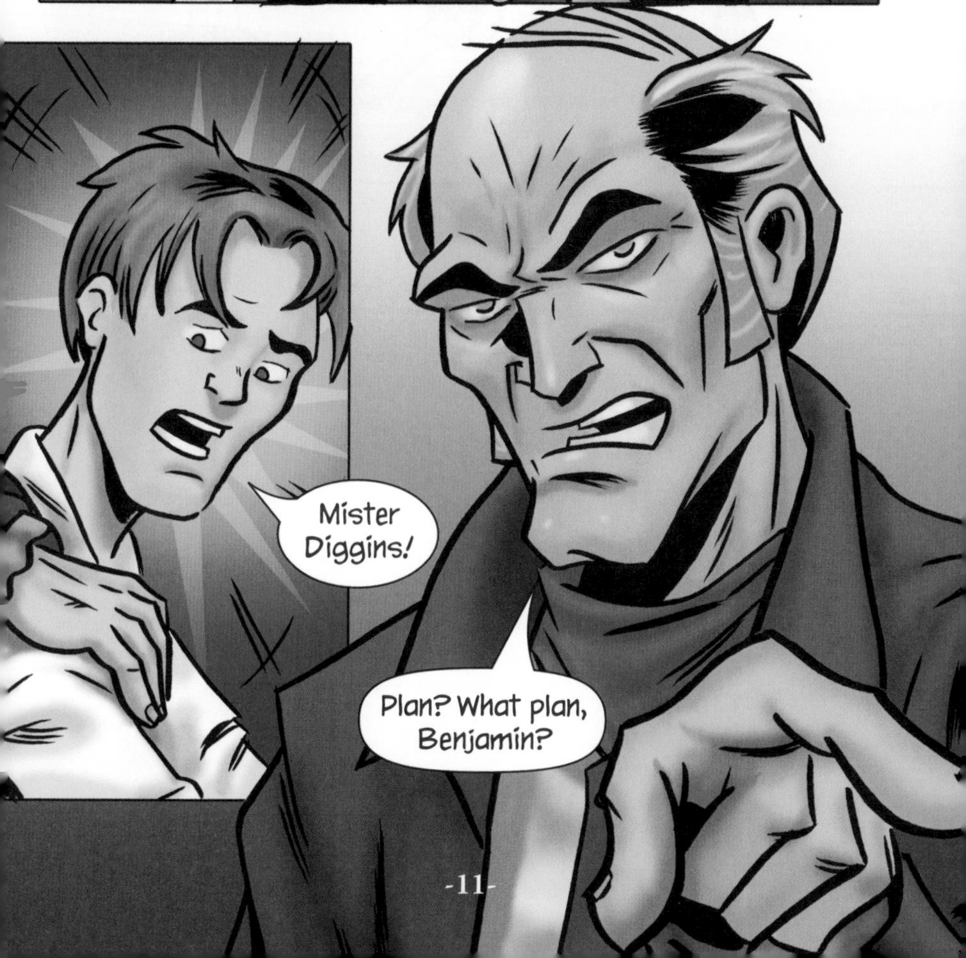
Mister Diggins!
Plan? What plan, Benjamin?

Diggins is my master. I'm an apprentice at his rope-making shop. I know everything there is to know about ropes. I know how to tie every knot in the book. I've learned the square knot, the slipknot, the hitch and half-hitch, for starters.

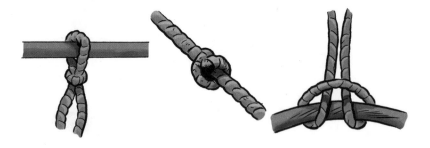

I love ropes, but I don't love Diggins. He's a Loyalist through and through! If he finds out what we're up to, he'll run straight to the British and warn them.

I can't let that happen.

When we get home, I explain to Diggins that nothing is going on. But try as I might, I can't make him believe me. Now, I'm in a bind of my own.

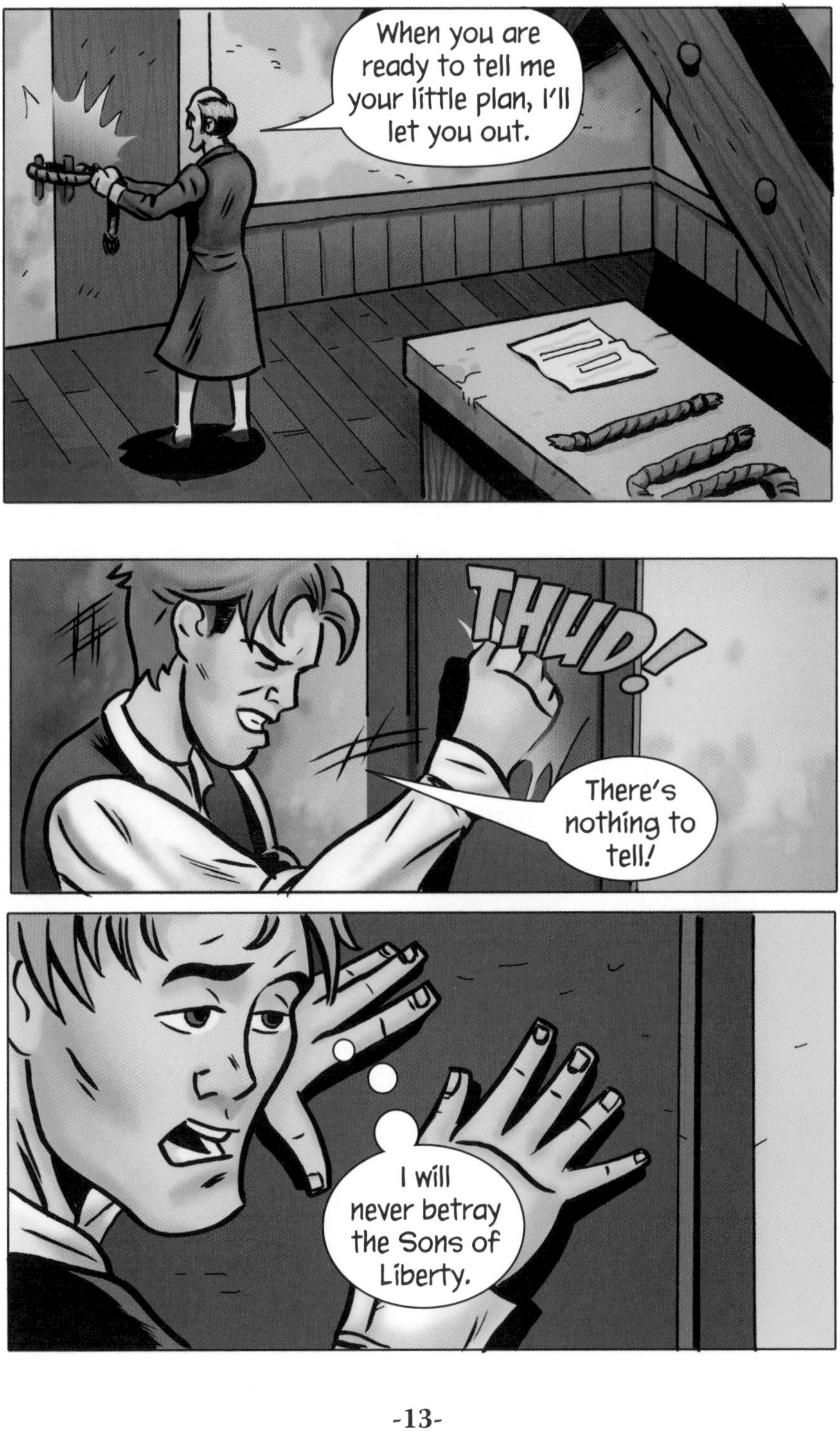
When you are ready to tell me your little plan, I'll let you out.
THUD!
There's nothing to tell!
I will never betray the Sons of Liberty.

Chapter 2

THE ESCAPE

As good as I am with ropes, Diggins is better. He has tied a knot so tight it will take a hundred years to loosen it. I am a prisoner in my room. Diggins shoves pieces of bread under the door. He's trying to force me to tell him the plan.

At six o'clock tonight, Samuel Adams and the rest of the rebels will march to Griffin's Wharf and dump the tea into the water. The British are about to learn a lesson they'll never forget!

The sky outside my window darkens. If only I could be heading toward Griffin's Wharf, too.

As the clock strikes five, I make a decision.

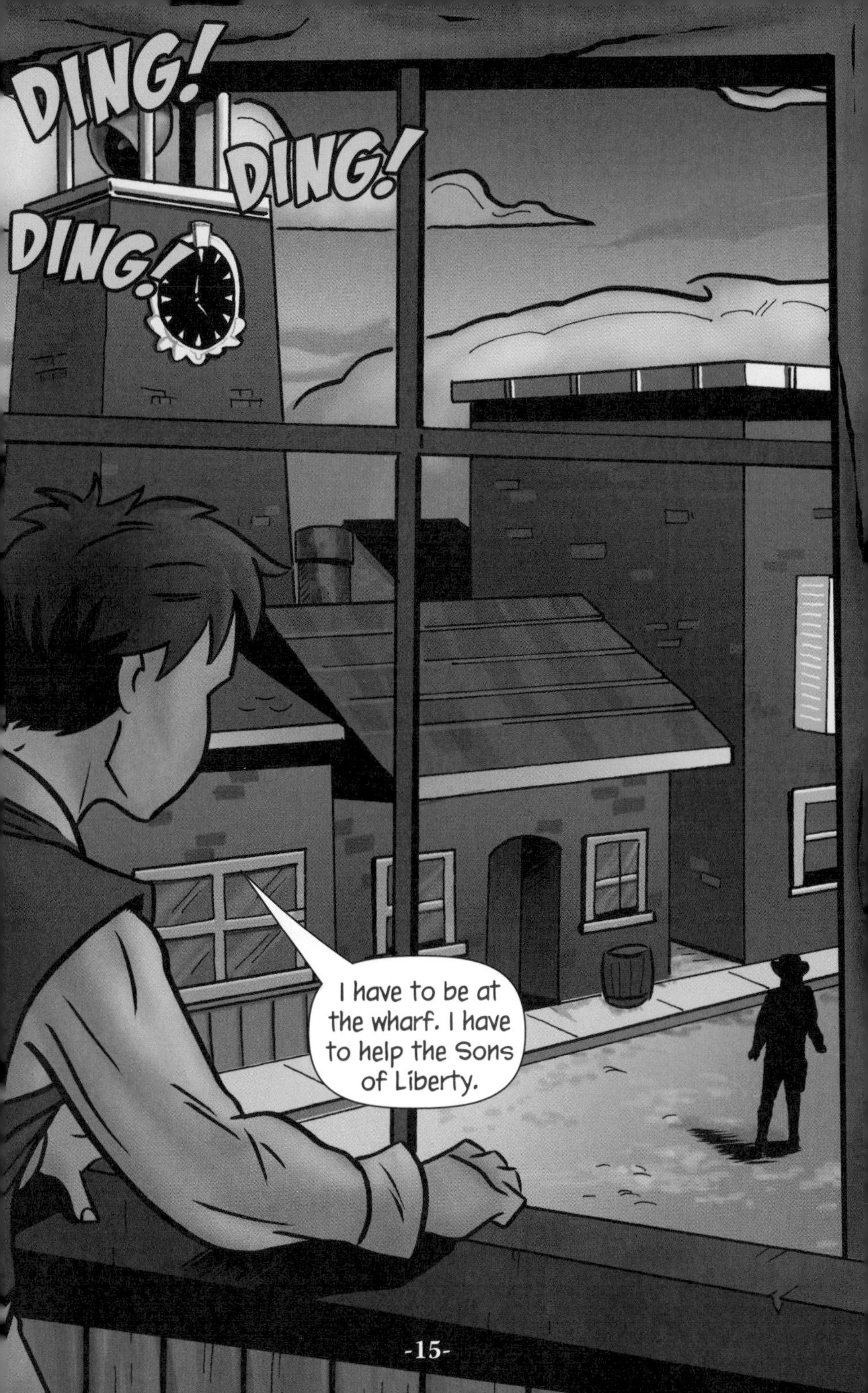
DING!
DING!
DING!
I have to be at the wharf. I have to help the Sons of Liberty.

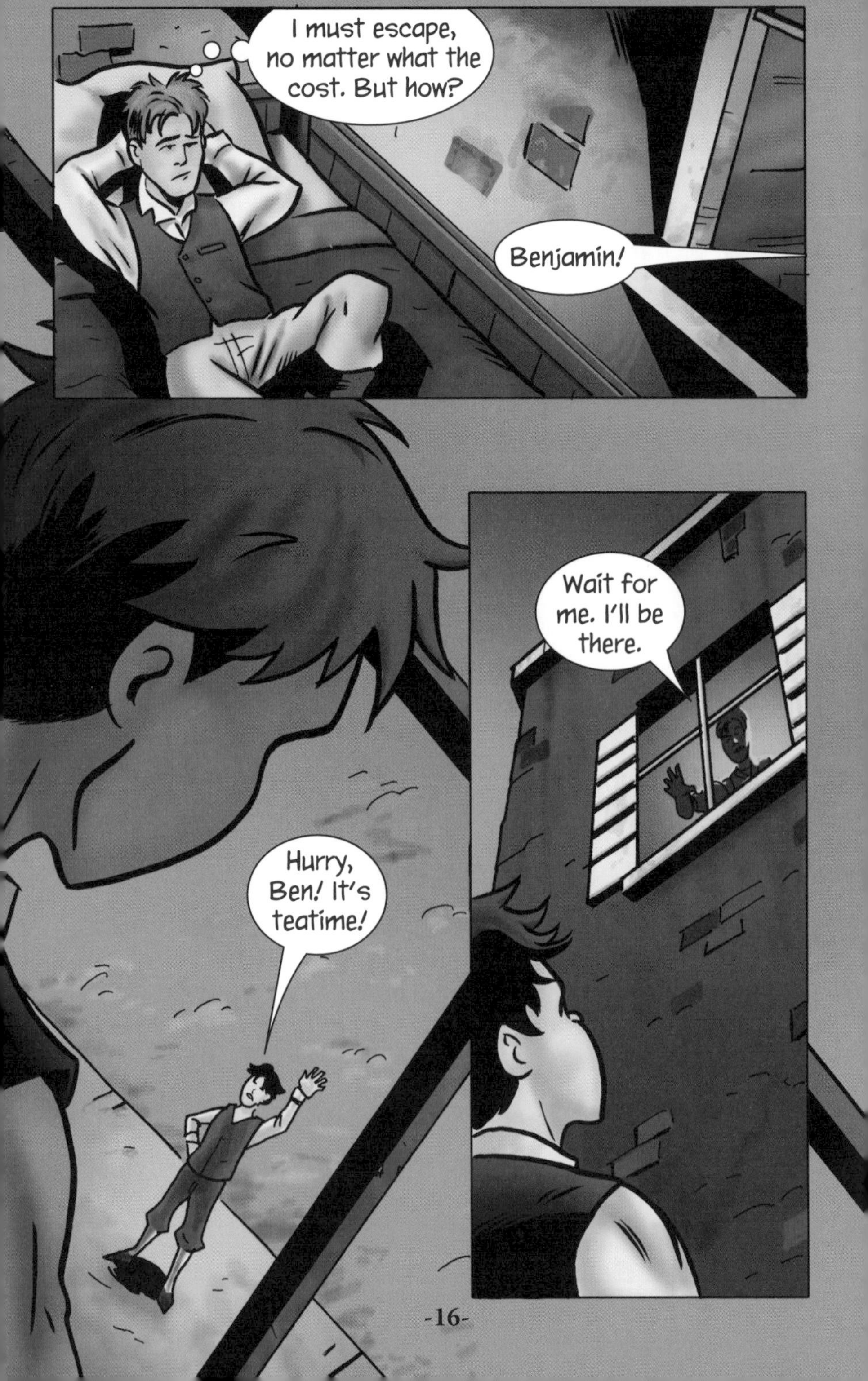
I must escape, no matter what the cost. But how?
Benjamin!
Wait for me. I'll be there.
Hurry, Ben! It's teatime!

I search my room for something to break the door open. All I have is a picture frame, a Bible, a candle, and a change of clothes.

Nothing.

I sit down on the bed. I don't want to give up, but what else can I do? The window is too high to jump. I'll break my legs. Then what good will I be?

I decide to give Diggins one more shot. I pound on the door and shout with all the power in my lungs. "Mister Diggins! Release me right now!"

No answer.

"Diggins! I will tell you the plan, I promise. Just let me out!"

There's still nothing but silence. Where could old Diggins be? He must be gone.

I leap from the bed. If Diggins isn't here, then he must be on his way to warn the British.

I search the room one more time. Bible, picture frame, clothes, my creaky bed —

I give a whoop of joy. That's it! The answer has been under me the whole time.

I pull the sheets from the bed and spread one on the floor. Then, with all my strength, I rip the sheet into three long strips. I do the same with the other two sheets.

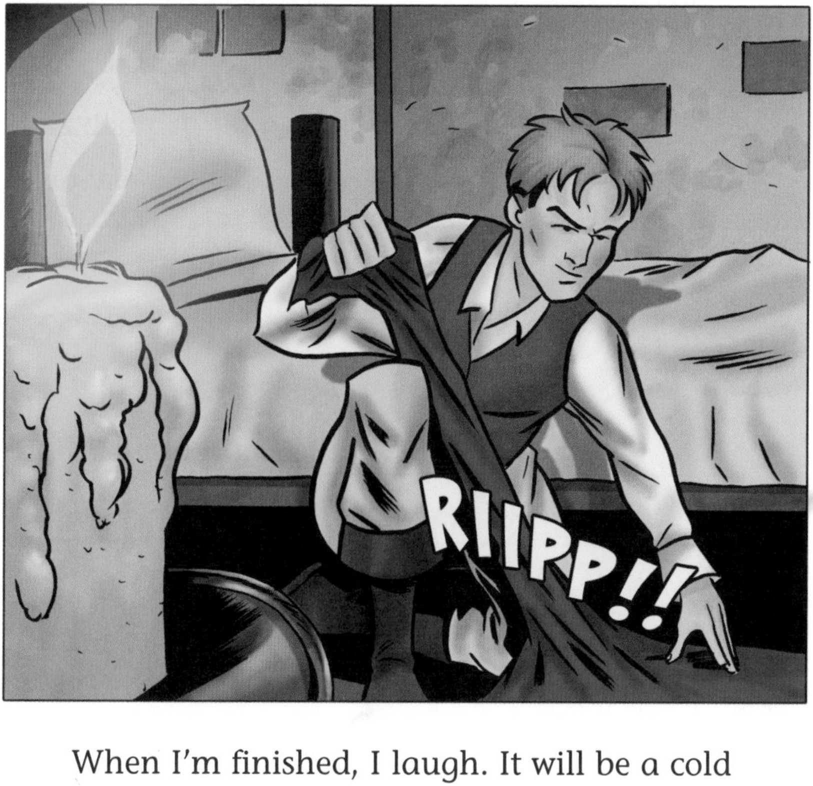
RIIPP!!

When I'm finished, I laugh. It will be a cold night without bed sheets. But hopefully my solution will work.

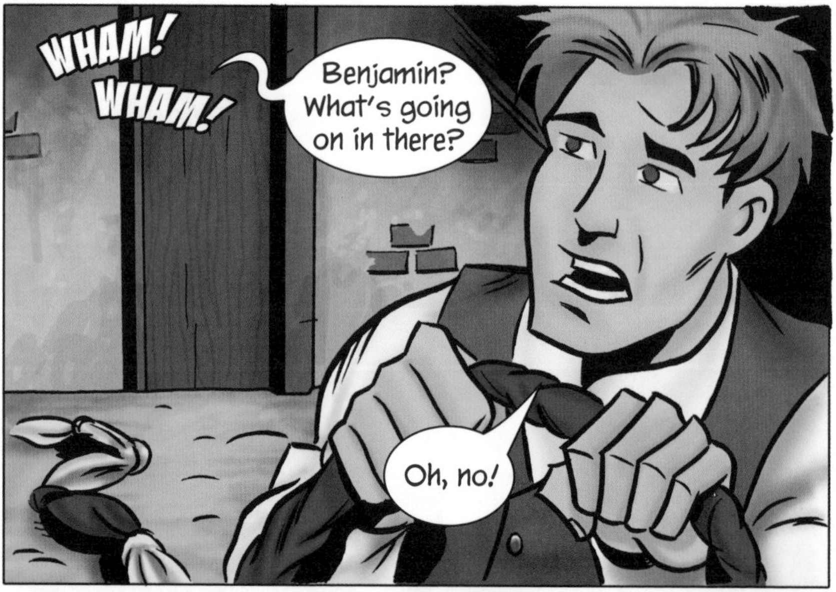
WHAM!
WHAM!
Benjamin? What's going on in there?
Oh, no!

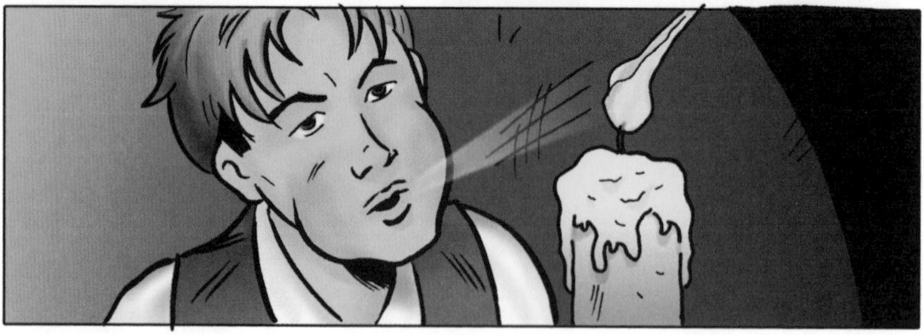

Diggins! What is he doing back so soon?

"I'm sleeping, Mr. Diggins. Do you need something?" I answer quietly. Then, I add, "There's nothing else to do in this prison."

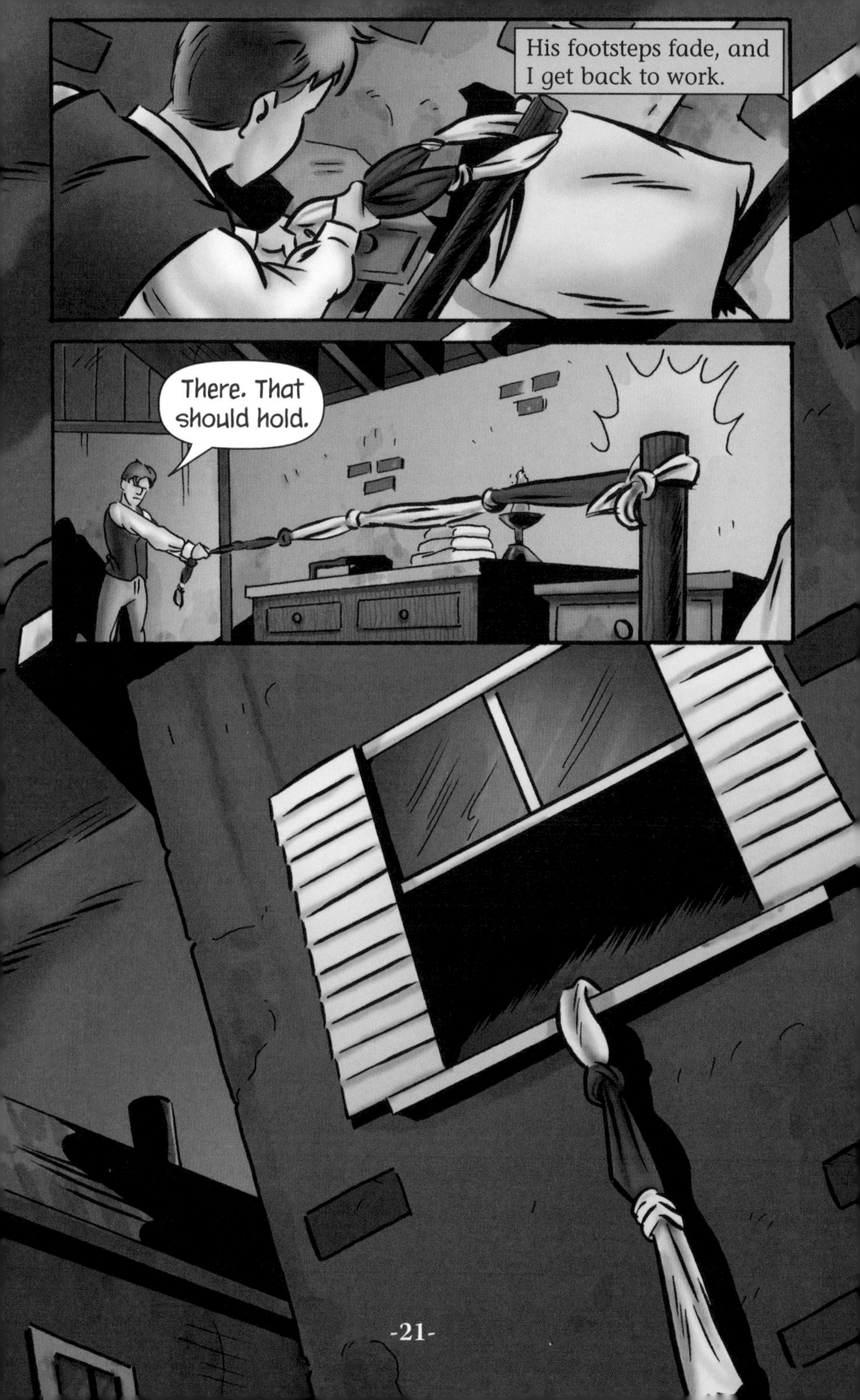

His footsteps fade, and I get back to work.
There. That should hold.

Outside, a cold rain is falling. I crawl out the window, holding the rope. I'm afraid to look down. It is a long way to fall.

I cling to the rope and lower myself inch by inch down the building. The rain has made the sheets slippery. I am scared, but I just keep thinking about the Sons of Liberty. The thought gives me courage.

I finally reach the ground and breathe a sigh of relief. I made it! My hands are a little sore, but I did it all on my own.

Now, I need to hurry. A shout suddenly stops me in my tracks.

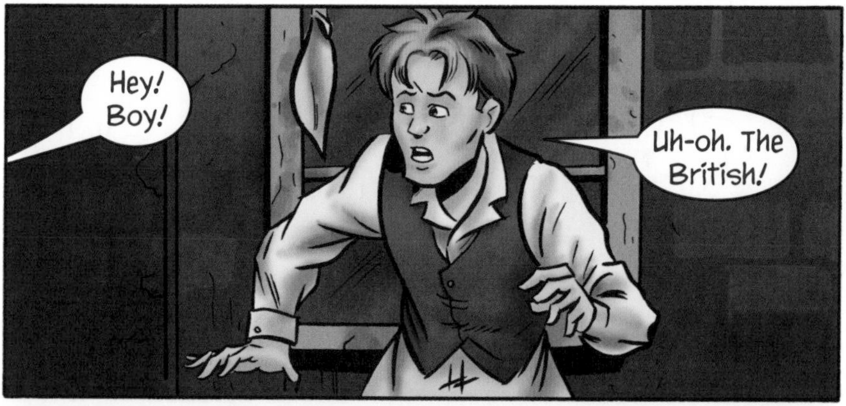
Hey! Boy!
Uh-oh. The British!

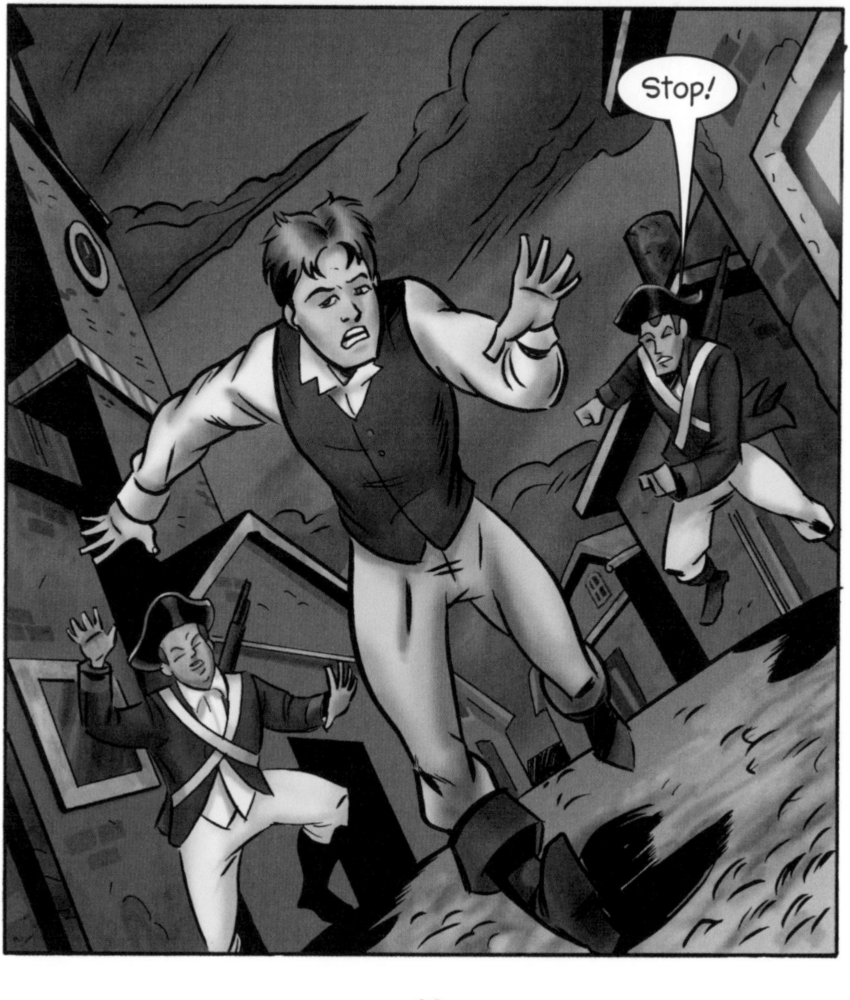
Stop!

Chapter 3
SALTWATER TEA

I run as fast as my shaking legs will move. My heart is pounding and my stomach is tied in a dozen sailor's knots. I know Joseph is waiting for me at the blacksmith's shop near the wharf. But I can't show up with two redcoats on my tail. The whole plan would be ruined.

I look back. The soldiers are gaining on me. Suddenly, I trip and fall onto the street, scraping my sore hands. Maybe Diggins was right to tie my door shut. If I had stayed in the room, none of this would be happening.

No! Sam Adams would never give up. I pick myself up and run even faster. The soldiers are still behind me, so I duck into an alley.

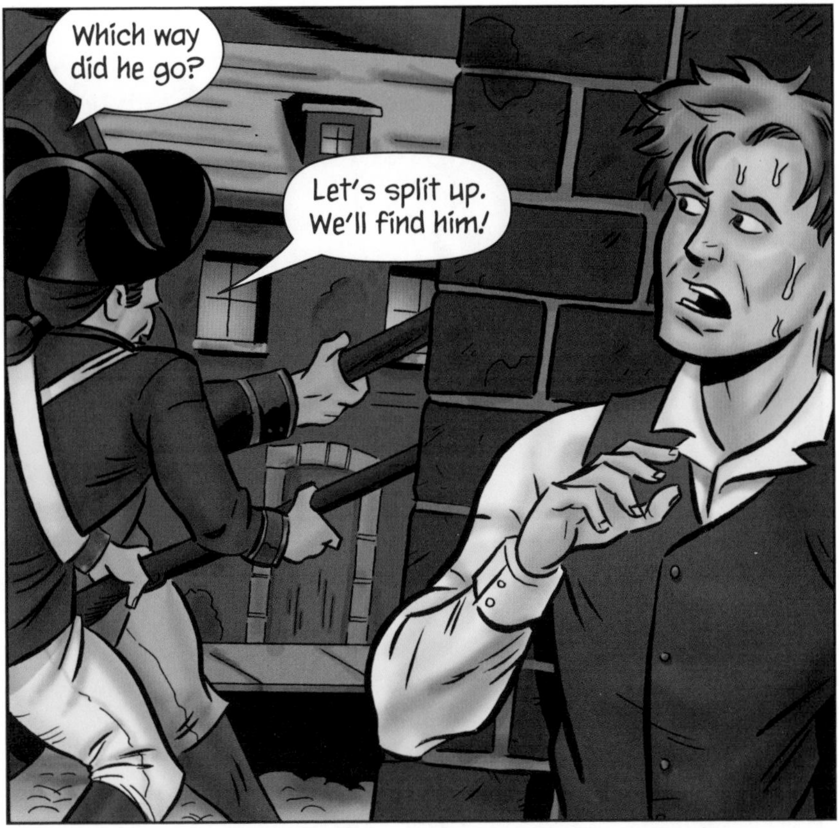
Which way did he go?
Let's split up. We'll find him!

Luckily, the soldiers run past me in the dark, and they don't even look my way.

When all that's left of them is a few slushy footprints, I slip out of my hiding spot and run toward the blacksmith's shop. Joseph and the Sons of Liberty will be waiting for me there. I just hope I'm not too late.

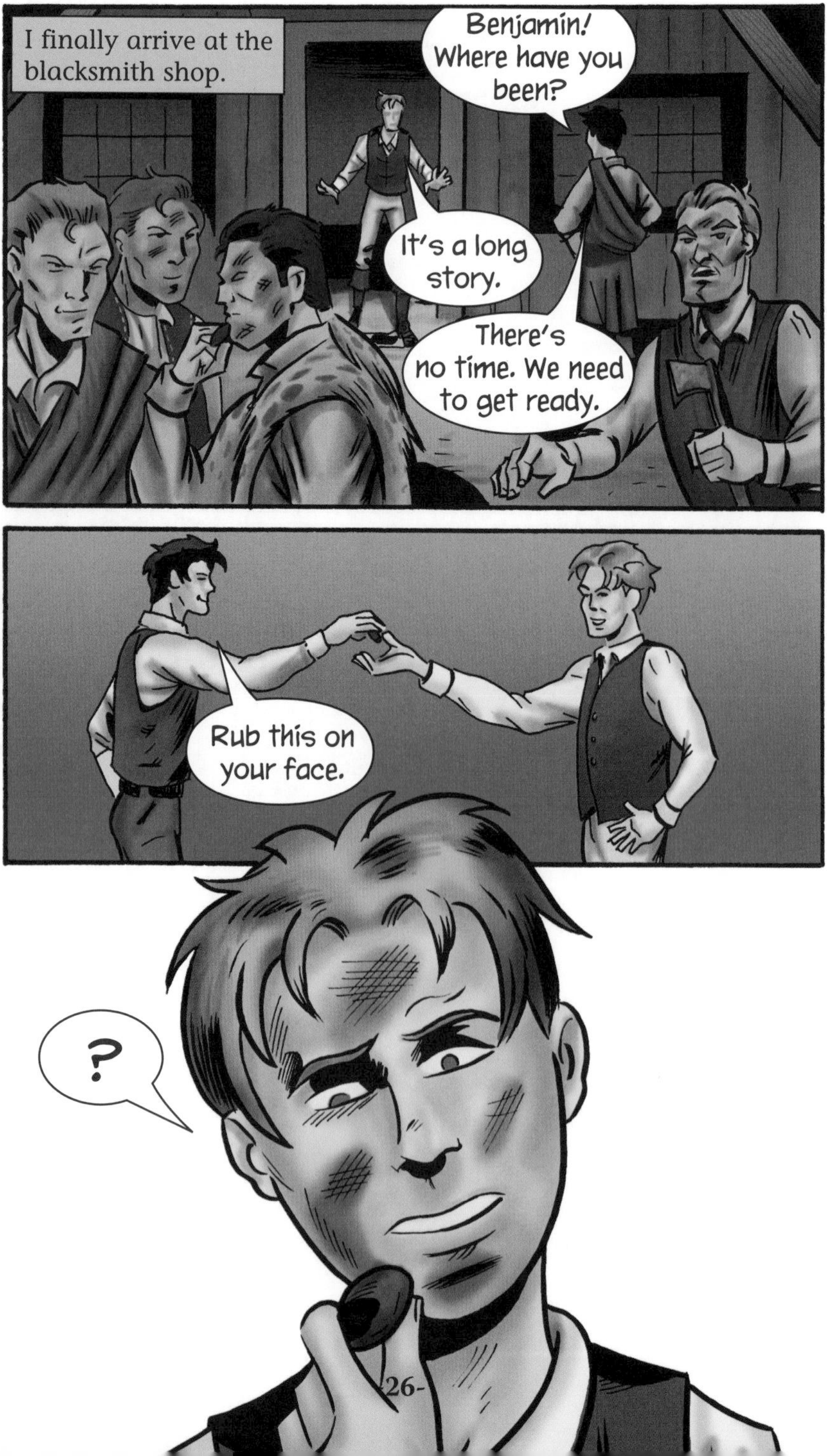
I finally arrive at the blacksmith shop.
Benjamin! Where have you been?
It's a long story.
There's no time. We need to get ready.
Rub this on your face.
?

I smear the charcoal on my face and wrap a blanket over my shoulders. Because of our Mohawk Indian disguise, the British won't be able to identify us.

As I'm putting on the last of my disguise, a tall man walks toward me. "Ready to be a Patriot?" he says.

Even though he is in disguise, I know the man's voice. It is none other than Samuel Adams himself.

"Yes, sir," I stutter.

I think he might tell me I'm too young, but he doesn't. Mr. Adams turns to the crowd gathered in the dark blacksmith shop. "Is everyone here loyal to the cause for liberty?" he shouts.

"Aye!" we reply.

Then he looks at Joseph and me. "Be careful tonight, boys," he says.

Chapter 4

OVERBOARD!

The masts of the three ships, the *Dartmouth*, the *Beaver*, and the *Eleanor*, rise against the night sky. Our feet thunder on the cobblestone road as we near the harbor.

Out of the corner of my eye I see the red of a British soldier uniform. It's the same soldier that chased me earlier. I give him a cheery wave.

"Hey!" he hollers. But he makes no move to chase us. He stands with the other redcoats. They all look confused at our huge group.

"They're no match for us!" Joseph says.

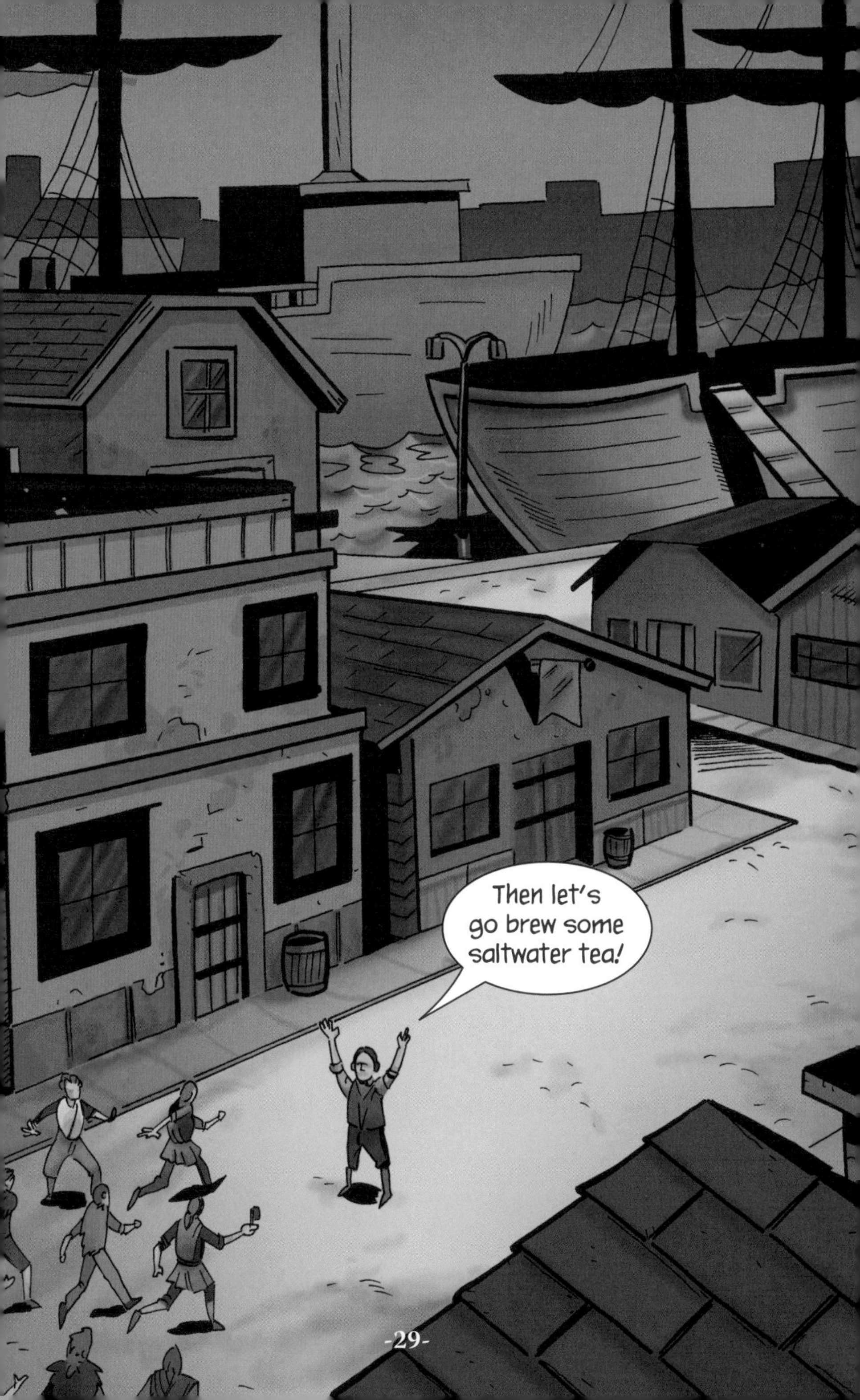
Then let's go brew some saltwater tea!

We march past Old South Church, where a town meeting is being held. When the townspeople see us, they cheer. They pour out of the doors of the church and fall in line behind us, cheering and waving us on.

A wave of pride overtakes me. Tonight, the whole town of Boston is on our side.

The whole town except one person — Diggins.

The thought of Diggins burns away all fear and coldness inside me. I wonder what he's doing now. Probably searching high and low for me.

We reach the dock. The other rebels scramble toward the ships.

"Which one should we board first?" I ask Joseph.

"There! The *Eleanor*," replies Joseph.

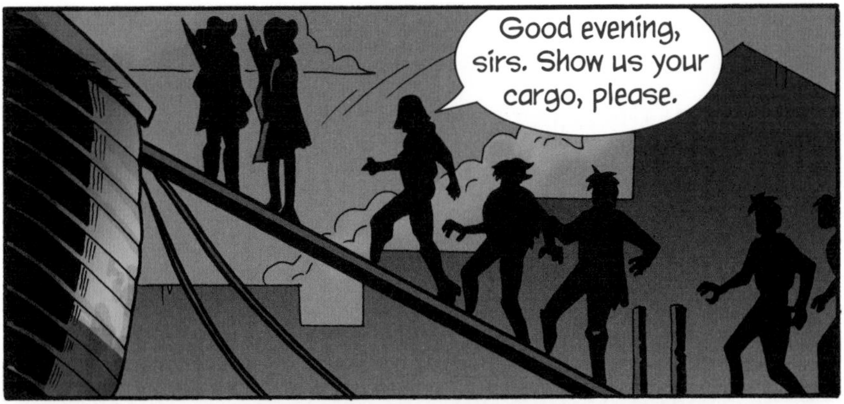
Good evening, sirs. Show us your cargo, please.

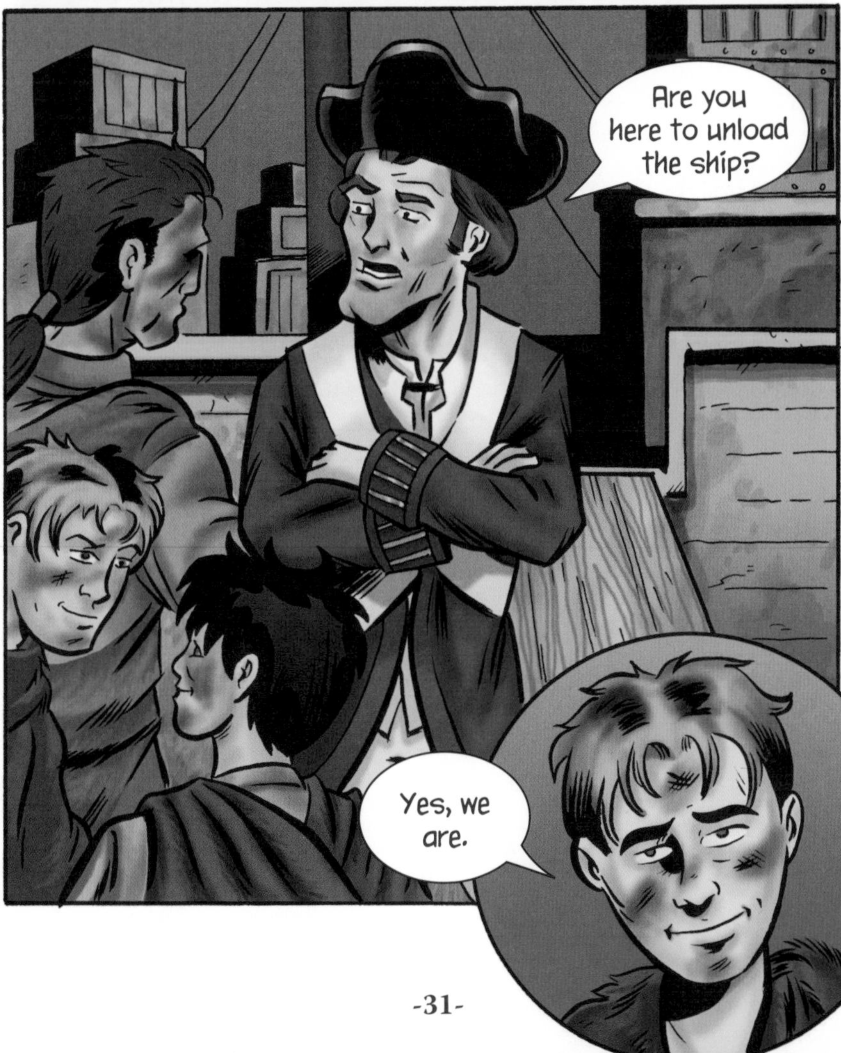
Are you here to unload the ship?
Yes, we are.

One of the sailors points the way to the cargo hold.

"Stay here," I command Joseph. "I'll lift the crates to you."

I climb into the hold and try to lift a crate of tea. It won't budge. It is heavier than I thought.

"Let me help you with that," says a soft voice. The voice sounds familiar, but the hold is so dark I can't see who it is.

Then it hits me. It must be Sam Adams!

Together, we lift the crate onto the deck. Soon we are joined by other disguised rebels. In minutes we've cleared the hold.

"Time to go overboard!" shouts the man next to me. We climb to the deck, and the party begins.

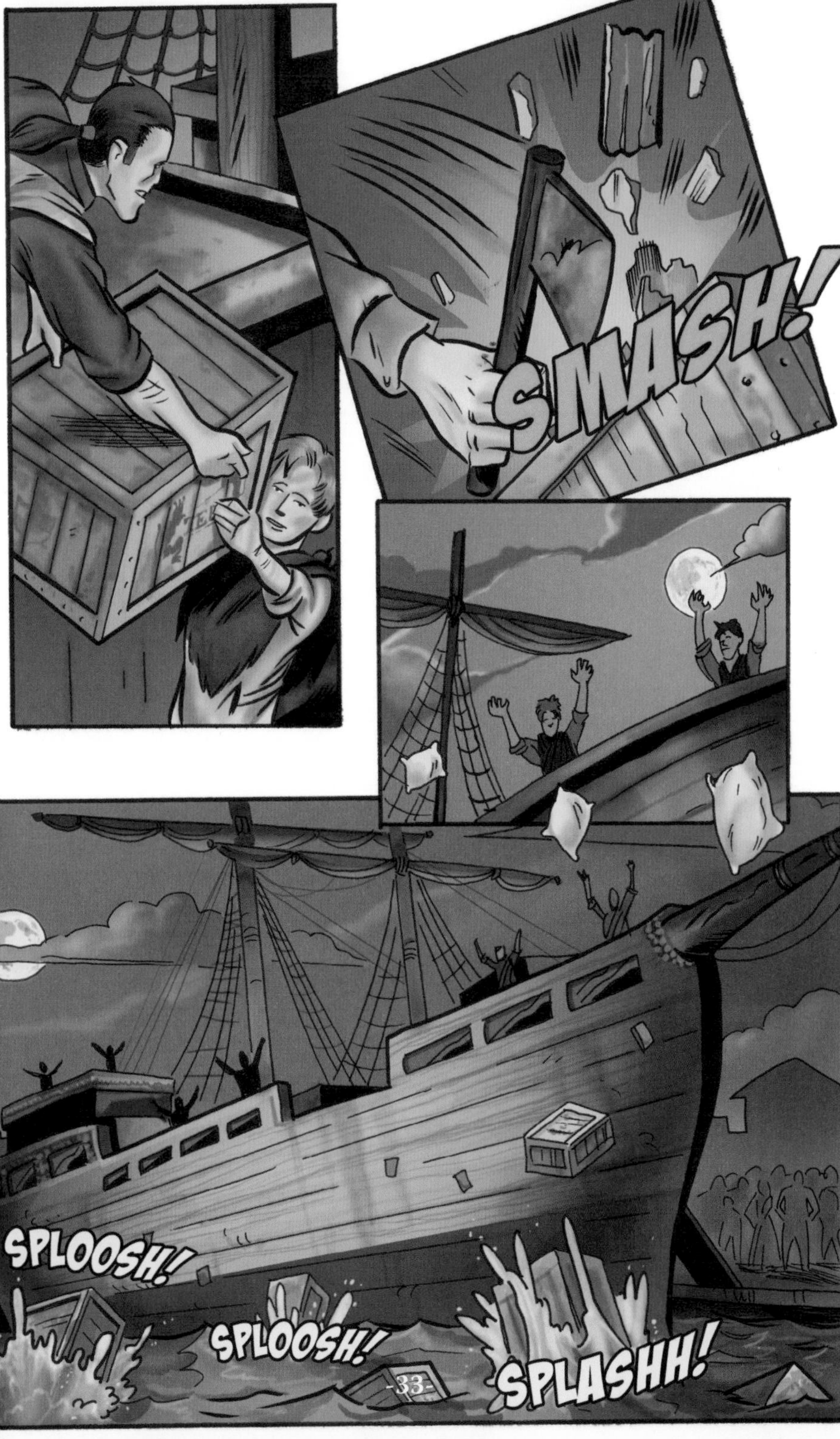
SMASH!
SPLOOSH!
SPLOOSH!
SPLASHH!

The air is cold. My skin is soaked with sweat. But the sound of the tea hitting the water urges me on. From now on, the British will know they can't boss us colonists around.

The crowd cheers from the shore. A few British soldiers stand about, uncertain what to do. They look like they are waiting for orders. I pause and tug Joseph's shirt.

"Look at those redcoats!" I laugh.

Joseph laughs. "They'll never do anything with this crowd."

"There must be seven thousand people on the shore!" I say.

A shout interrupts us.

Benjamin! Watch out!

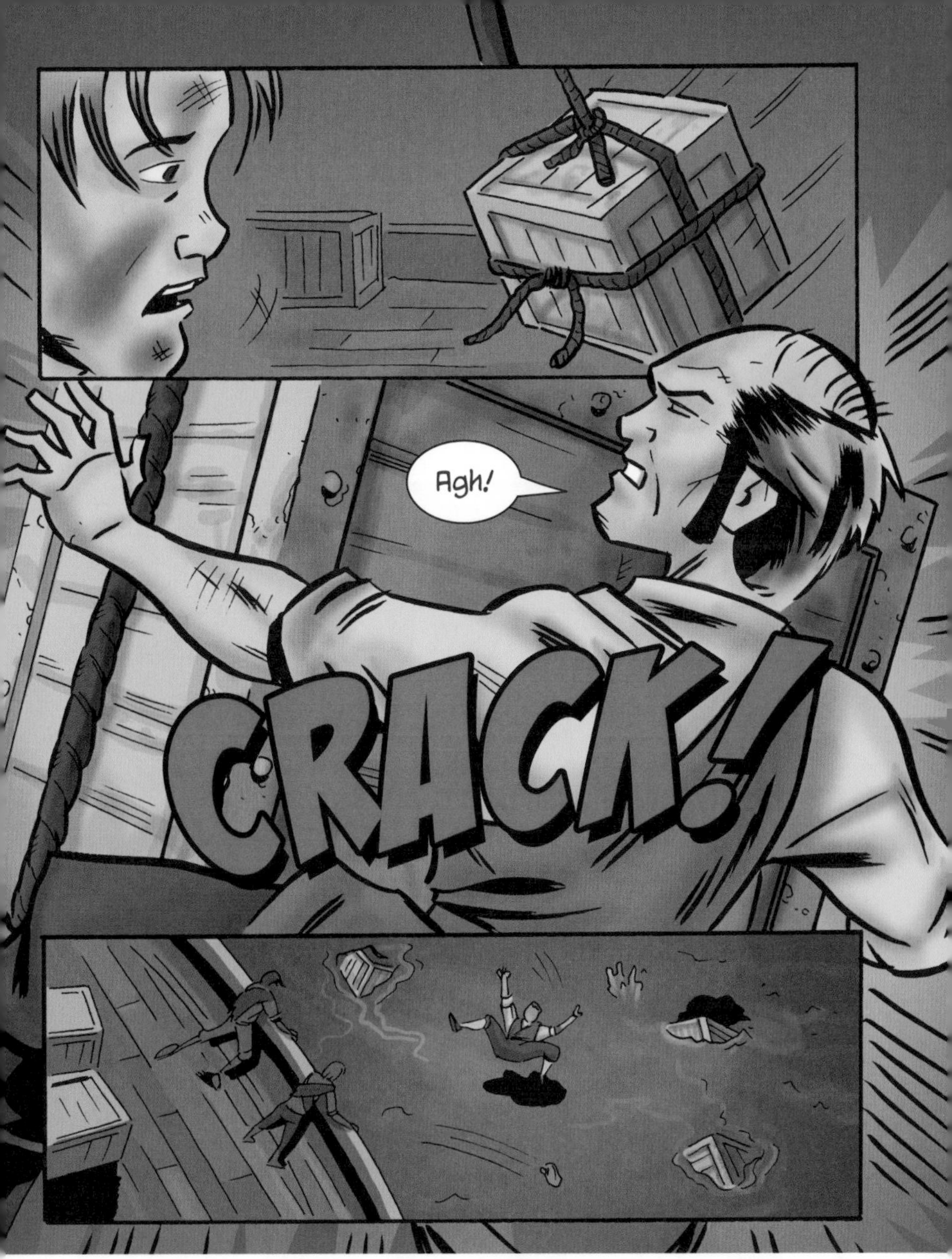
Agh!
CRACK!

"Man overboard!" I shout for help, but no one seems to hear me above the breaking crates.

"We have to help him," I yell to Joseph as I stare into the dark water below.

The man's shout saved my life. Now I have to save his. Not thinking, I make a sudden decision.

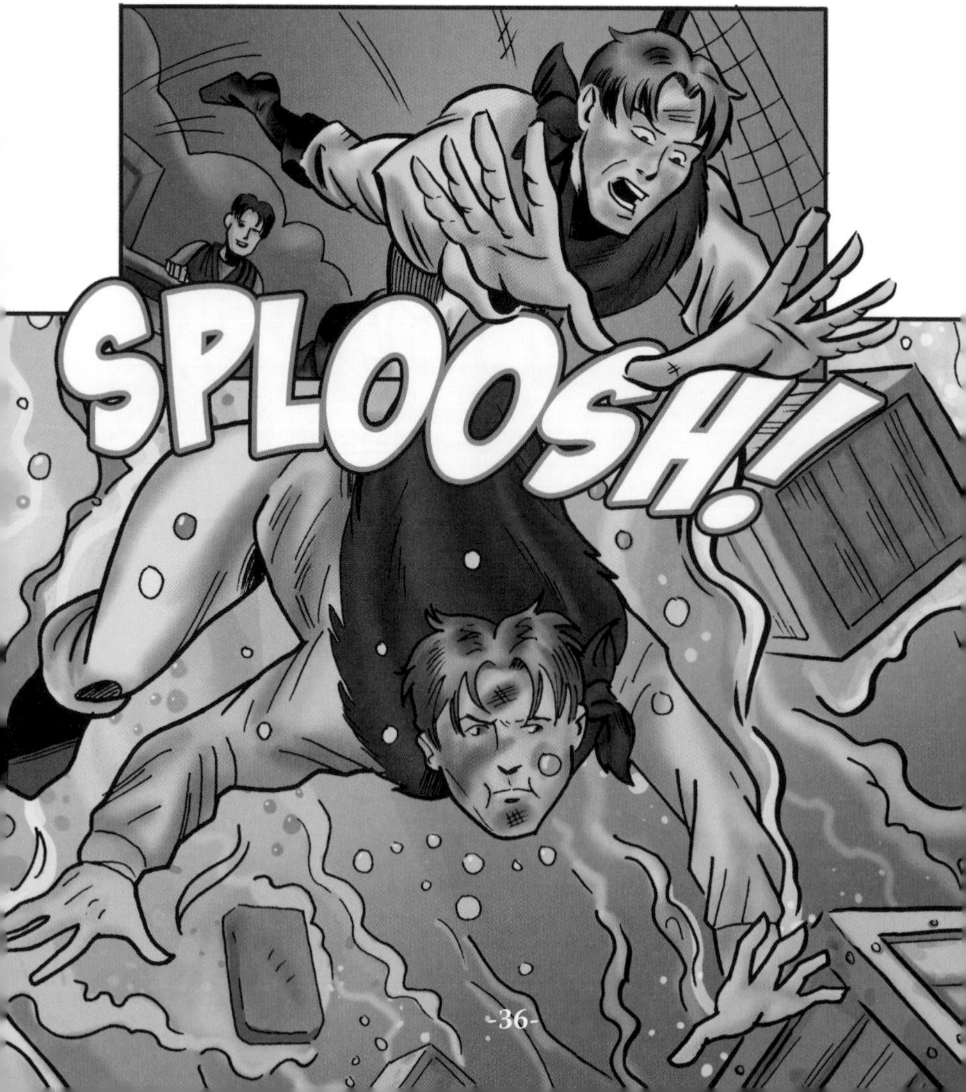
SPLOOSH!

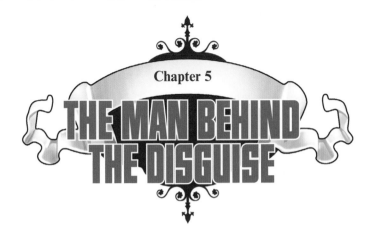

Chapter 5
THE MAN BEHIND THE DISGUISE

I finally break the surface of the water. Around me tea and crates are falling. I duck my head underwater, barely missing a flying crate.

The water is dark and cold. I look around me, but I can't see the man.

Hello?

I hear a splash near the boat. "Hello?" I call again, swimming toward the sound. My clothes are heavy with water and tea.

A wave splashes against my face and into my mouth. I spit out the water. Yuck! I never have liked tea.

A shape splashes toward me. "Benjamin?" the shape calls.

Joseph! It is Joseph. He has jumped in after me. But where is the man who saved me?

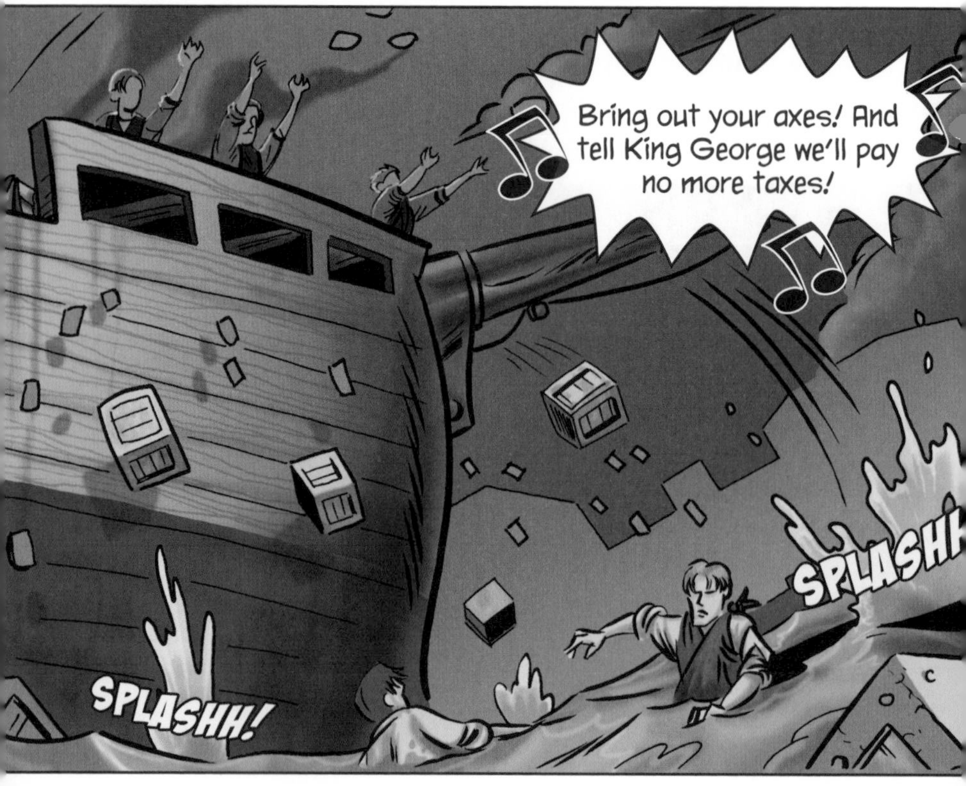
Bring out your axes! And tell King George we'll pay no more taxes!
SPLASH!
SPLASHH!

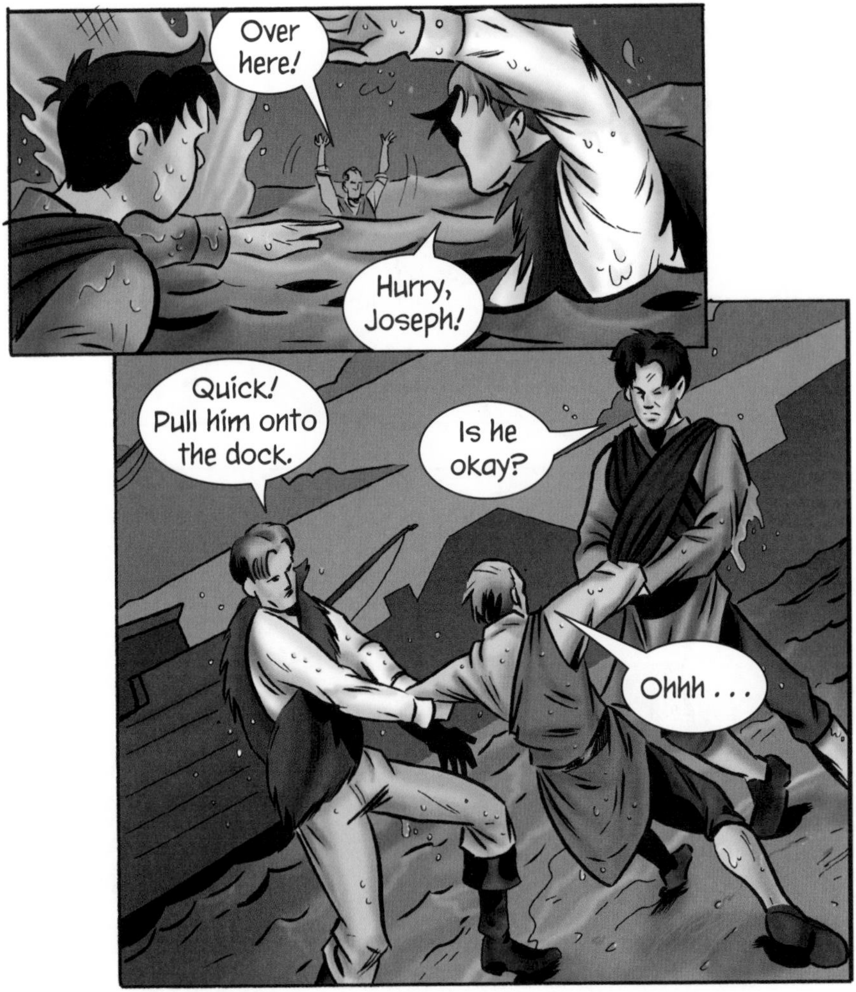
Over here!
Hurry, Joseph!
Quick! Pull him onto the dock.
Is he okay?
Ohhh . . .

The charcoal and paint have washed off the man's face. As we pull him to shore, I take a good look at him. The sight almost makes me drop him back in the water.

He is not a Son of Liberty. Not even close.

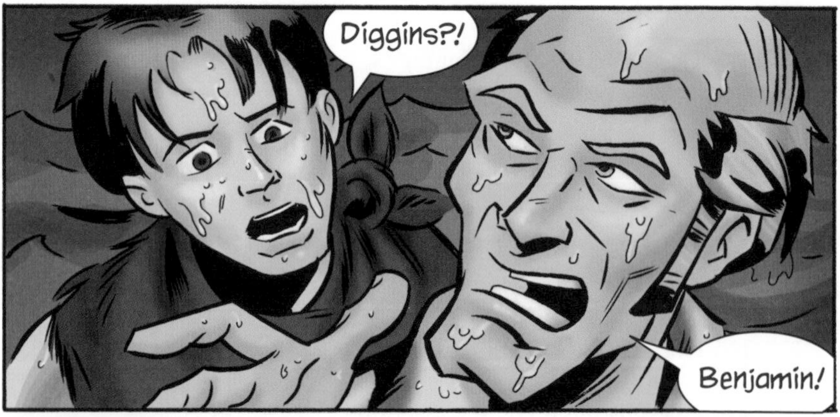
Diggins?!
Benjamin!

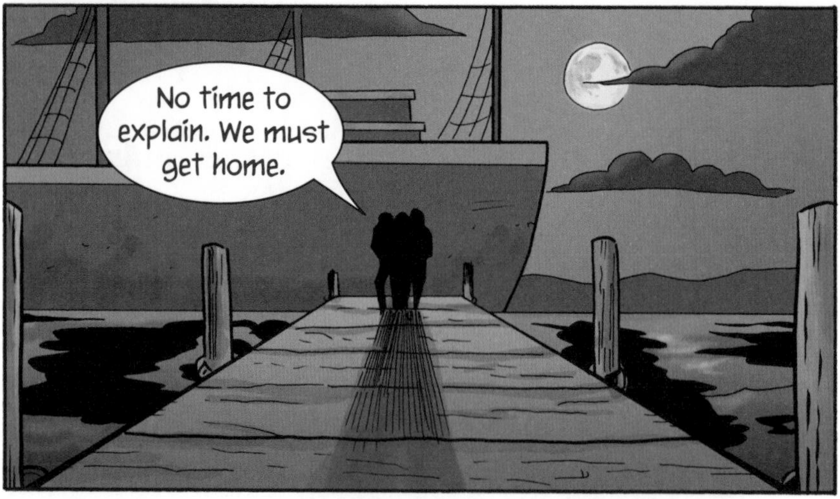
No time to explain. We must get home.

Diggins coughs. He keeps trying to talk, but I don't let him. He has to listen to me, for once.

We get him to his feet and push through the crowd. I take a look back at the wharf. The last of the tea has scattered to the fish. Our job is done.

Chapter 6

THE LOYALIST'S FATE

We leave a trail of saltwater tea on the street as we trudge toward the rope-making shop. Joseph keeps asking Diggins questions, but I tell him to be quiet. I need time to think things through on my own.

Why was Diggins helping with the tea party? Everyone knows he is a Loyalist. He doesn't want freedom from British rule. He has a painting of King George right in his shop.

There's only one answer. He was there to catch me. And now he'll throw me out on the streets.

We turn the corner near the shop. And there, we run into a wall of red.

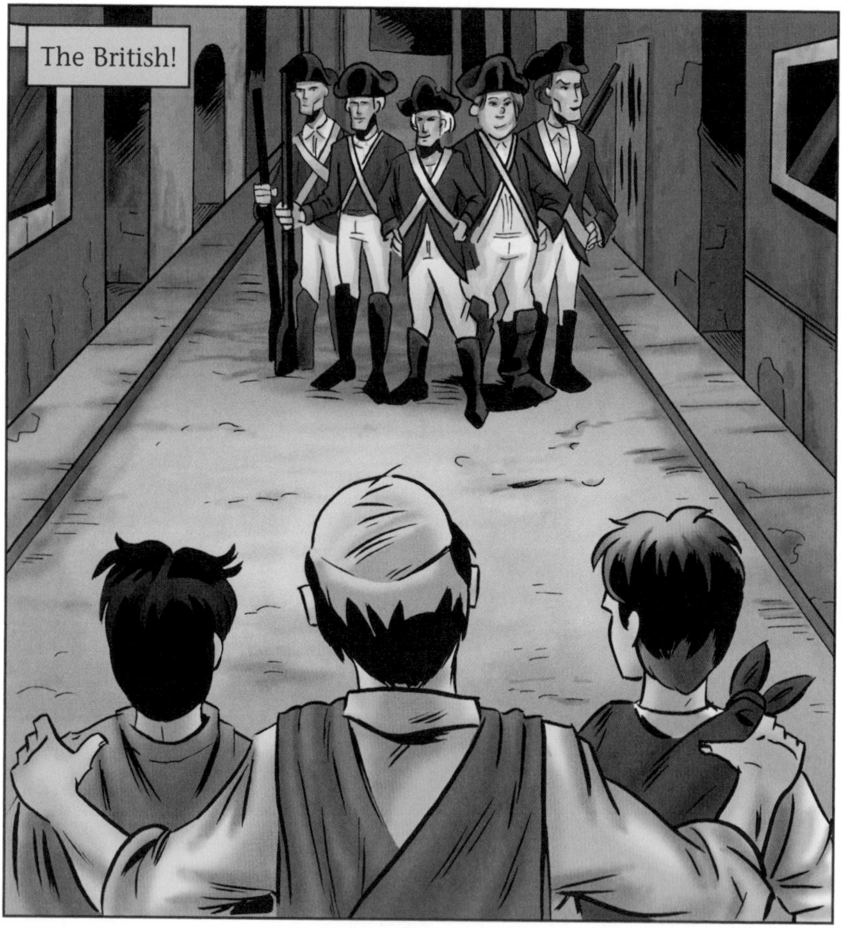
The British!

"Mr. Diggins!" one of the soldiers exclaims. "Why are you soaking wet?"

Diggins coughs. "I've been out in the rain all night," he says. "Looking for my young apprentice here."

The soldier raises an eyebrow at me.

"A girl," Diggins explains with a wink and chuckle. "He's in love!"

My face burns as red as the soldiers' uniforms. I turn my head to hide that I'm embarrassed. The soldiers laugh.

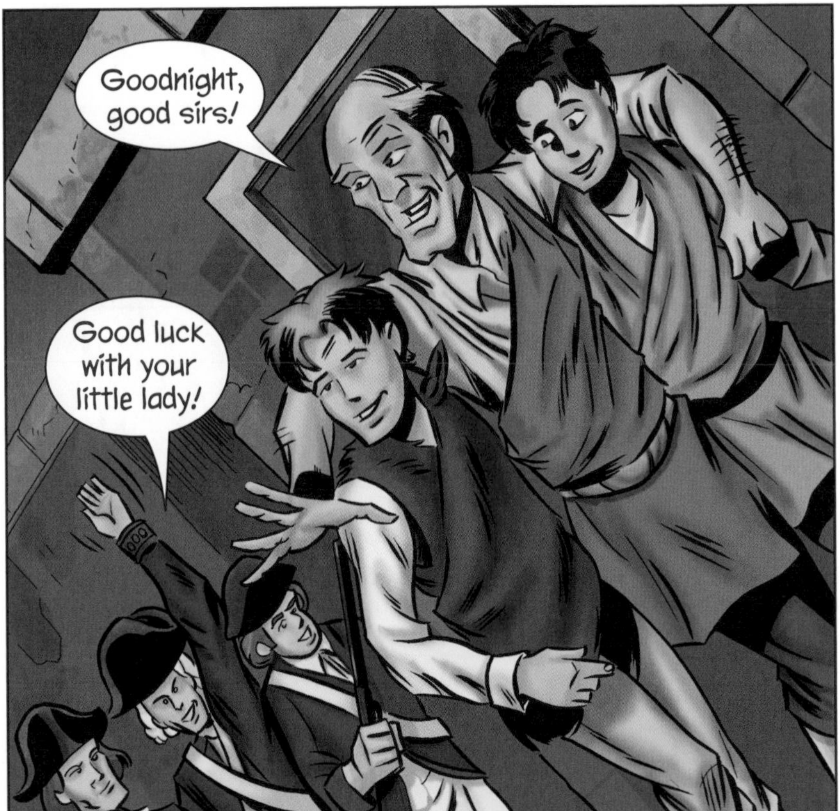
Goodnight, good sirs!
Good luck with your little lady!

Once again, we outsmarted the British. But I can't figure out why Diggins helped us. What's in it for him?

We stumble toward the shop. At the door, Joseph says good-bye and walks toward his home.

While Diggins is drying in front of the fire, I go to my room. I pack my belongings into a bag. I'm about to say good-bye to rope making forever.

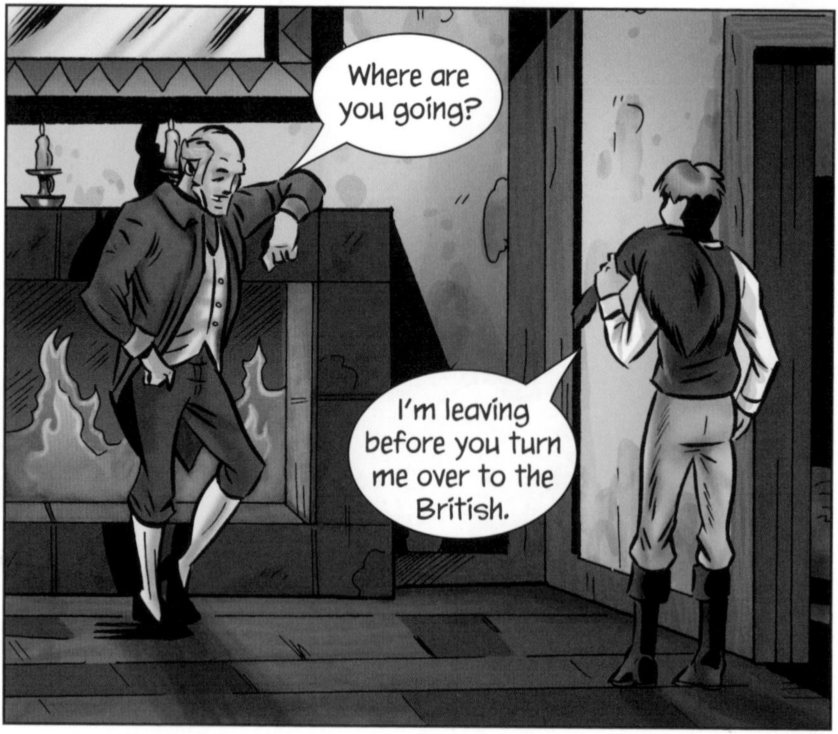
Where are you going?
I'm leaving before you turn me over to the British.

Diggins sighs. "I won't betray you, Benjamin."

"But you are a Loyalist!" I say.

"I was only pretending to be a Loyalist," he explains.

I am shocked. "But why?" I ask.

"I was afraid that if I joined the rebels, the British would take away my shop." Diggins looks around him. "And I love my shop."

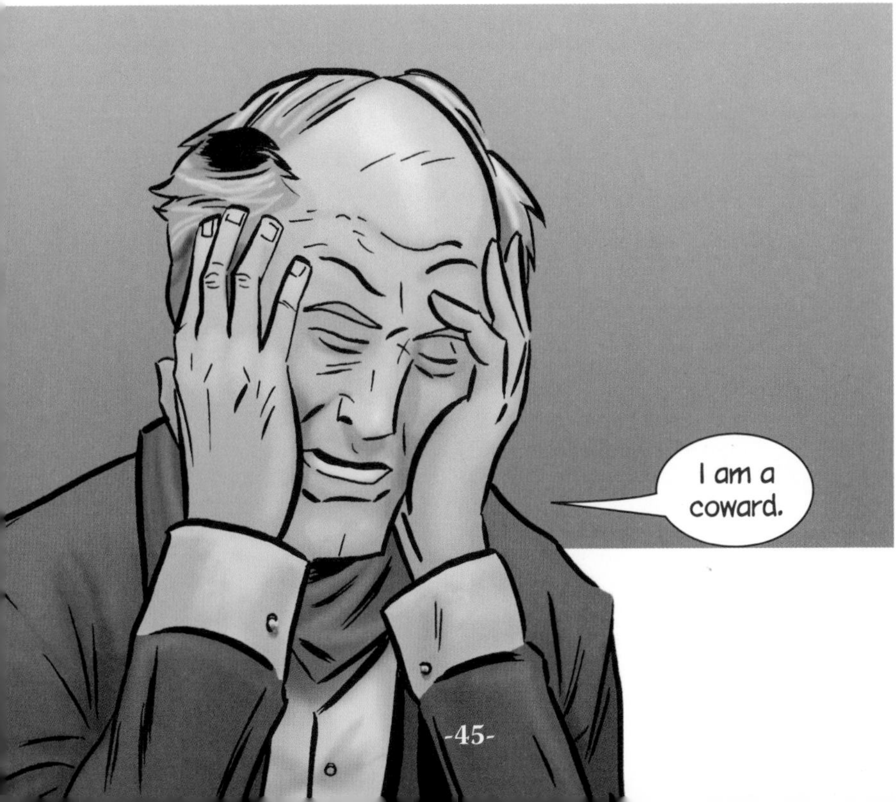
I am a coward.

So he wasn't at the wharf to catch me! I shake my head to clear the water from my ears. Am I hearing him right? Diggins, the Loyalist, is now a rebel?

"I went to the town meeting tonight," Diggins explains. "I saw how angry the tea tax made the townspeople. So I joined the party."

"Why did you lock me in my room?" I ask.

Diggins looks up at me and smiles. "I was afraid. I knew you were up to something. I didn't want you to be killed or captured."

I feel a new respect for Diggins. Tonight, he was willing to risk everything for liberty, even his beloved shop.

"You are not a coward," I tell him.

He gives me a smile of relief.

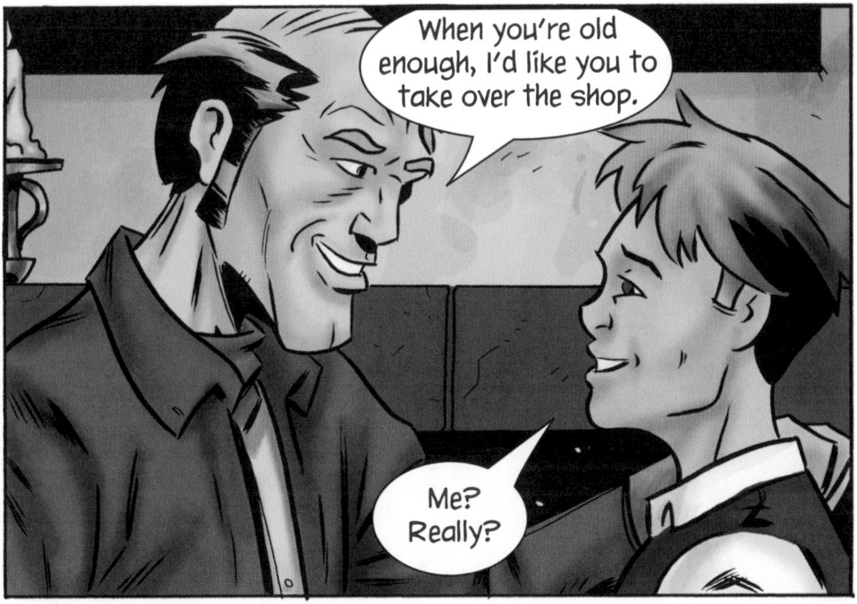
When you're old enough, I'd like you to take over the shop.
Me? Really?

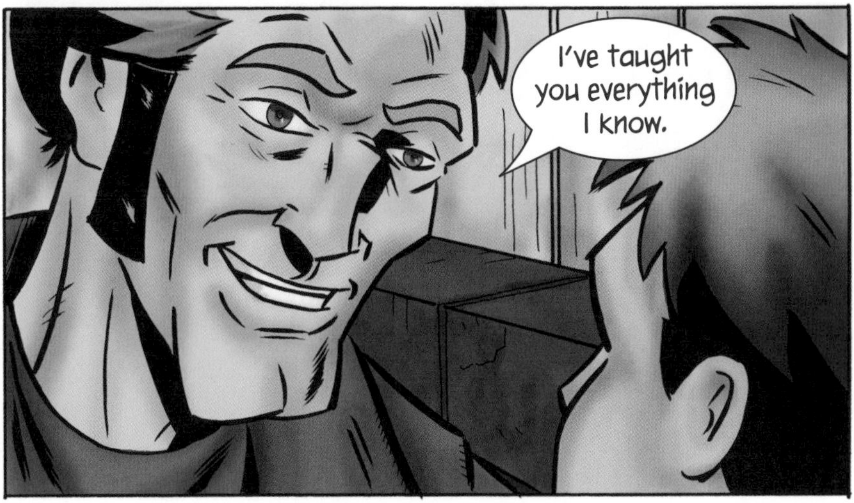
I've taught you everything I know.

I can't believe what I am hearing. Diggins isn't going to throw me out on the streets.

Outside, I hear the noise of the crowd. The rebels are coming back from the harbor, singing and shouting.

Go on! Join them!

I drop my bag and rush out into the street. Sam Adams is at the head of the crowd. He gives me a smile and tips his hat.

There's still one person missing from the celebration.

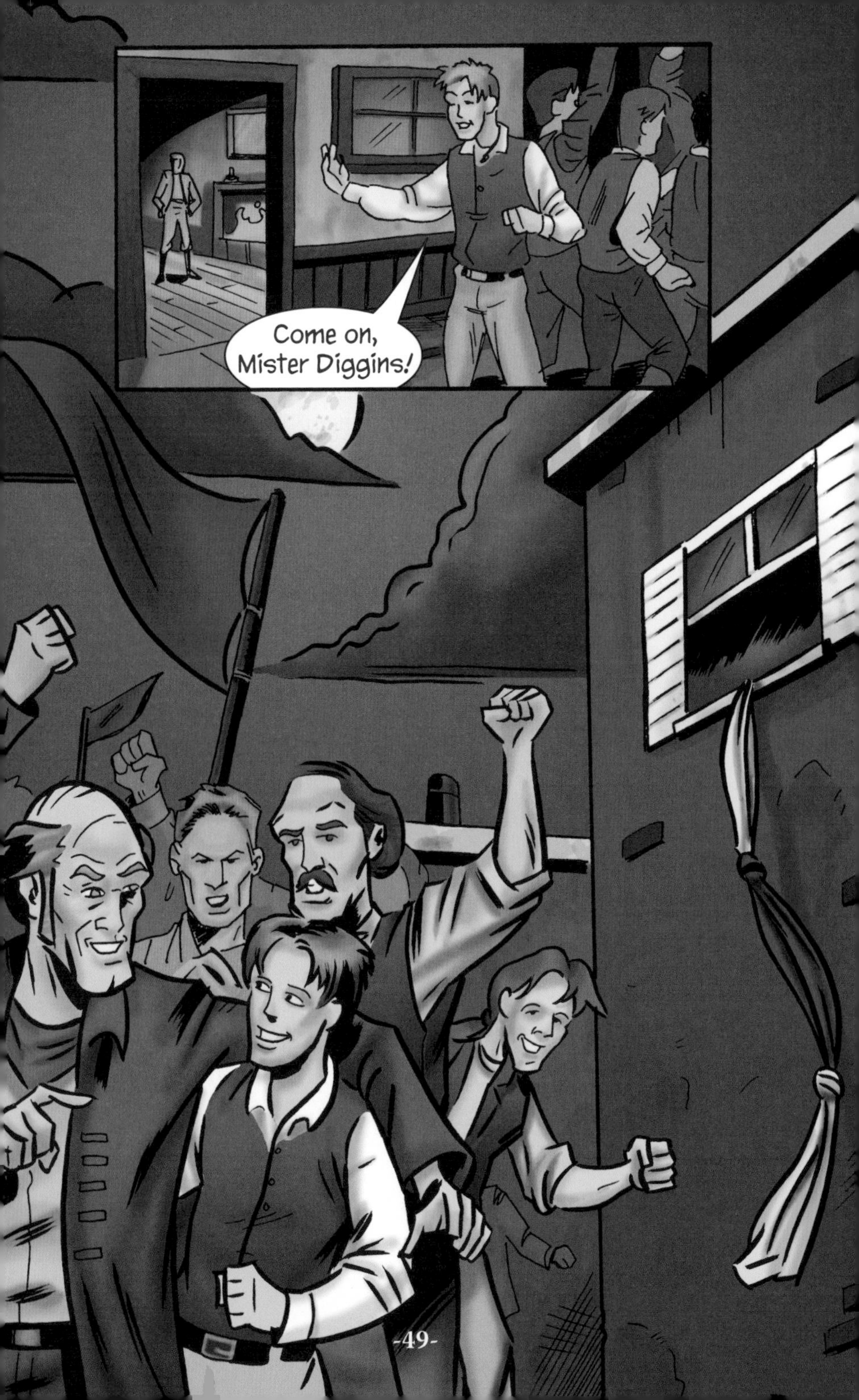
Come on, Mister Diggins!

ABOUT THE AUTHOR

Jessica Gunderson grew up in the small town of Washburn, North Dakota. She has a bachelor's degree from the University of North Dakota and a master's degree in creative writing from Minnesota State University, Mankato. She likes rainy days and thunderstorms. She also likes exploring haunted houses and playing *Mad Libs*. She teaches English in Madison, Wisconsin, where she lives with her cat, Yossarian.

ABOUT THE ILLUSTRATOR

Brent Schoonover has worked as a freelance illustrator since graduating from the Minneapolis College of Art and Design in 2002. He has illustrated for companies such as General Mills, Best Buy, Target, and Continental Airlines. He also worked on several graphic novels, including *Horrorwood*, published by Ape Entertainment in 2006, and several books by Capstone Press. Schoonover currently lives in St. Paul, Minnesota, with his wife, two cats, and one bulldog.

GLOSSARY

apprentice (uh-PREN-tiss)—a young person who learns a skill from a more experienced adult

betray (bi-TRAY)—to do something that hurts someone close to you, such as telling a secret

blacksmith (BLAK-smith)—someone who makes things made of iron, such as horseshoes

boycotting (BOI-kot-ing)—refusing to use a product to show disapproval for the maker

cloak (KLOHK)—a sleeveless coat that is wrapped around a person's shoulders like a cape

colonists (KOL-uh-nists)—people living in the 13 British colonies of North America

Loyalists (LOI-uhl-ists)—colonists that sided with the British during the American Revolution

Patriots (PAY-tree-uhts)—colonists against the British during the American Revolution

redcoats (RED-kohts)—British soldiers

tar and feather (TAHR AND FETH-ur)—to cover a person with tar and feathers as a punishment

wharf (WORF)—a dock for ships to unload cargo

MORE ABOUT THE BOSTON TEA PARTY

Two hundred men took part in the Boston Tea Party on December 16, 1773. Many of them were young apprentices, including 16 teenagers.

On that night, the Sons of Liberty dumped 342 crates of tea over the sides of the British ships *Dartmouth*, *Eleanor*, and *Beaver*. Weighing more than 45 tons (90,000 pounds), the tea floated onto the harbor shore for several weeks.

Although they ruined a lot of tea, protesters in the Boston Tea Party were careful not to damage or dirty anything else. Before they left the ships, the men even swept the decks clean.

Most people watching from shore cheered on the Sons of Liberty. In fact, the protest was so popular that colonists dumped even more tea off British ships on March 7, 1774.

The British weren't pleased with these protests. In today's money, the two events would have cost them more than 3 million dollars worth of tea.

The British Parliament decided that protests like the Boston Tea Party must be stopped. They passed a set of laws called the Intolerable Acts in 1774. The laws included closing the port of Boston until all the tea was paid for.

The Intolerable Acts only increased anger on both sides. In 1775, the American Revolutionary War began. A short time later, leaders of the 13 colonies officially declared their independence from Great Britain.

Samuel Adams, a leader of the Boston Tea Party, was one of 56 people to sign the Declaration of Independence on July 4, 1776.

DISCUSSION QUESTIONS

1. Benjamin snuck out of his room, even after Diggins told him to stay put. Do you think this was a good decision? Why or why not?

2. The Sons of Liberty destroyed nearly 90,000 pounds of British tea by dumping it into the harbor. Was this the right thing to do? Explain your answer.

3. If you lived in Boston, Massachusetts, during the late 1700s, which side would you have been on? Would you have protested with the colonists like Benjamin or sided with the British? Explain your answers.

WRITING PROMPTS

1. Young people often played important roles in historical events. Pick your favorite historical event. Then write a story with a kid as the hero.

2. Soon after the Boston Tea Party, colonists fought against Great Britain during the Revolutionary War (1775–1783). Describe what you think the characters in this story would have done during the war. Would Joseph fight for the Americans? Would Benjamin stay behind and work at the rope-making shop?

3. Benjamin came up with a clever way to escape from his bedroom. What if he hadn't thought of making a rope from the sheets? What other way could he have found to get out of that room? Write about it.

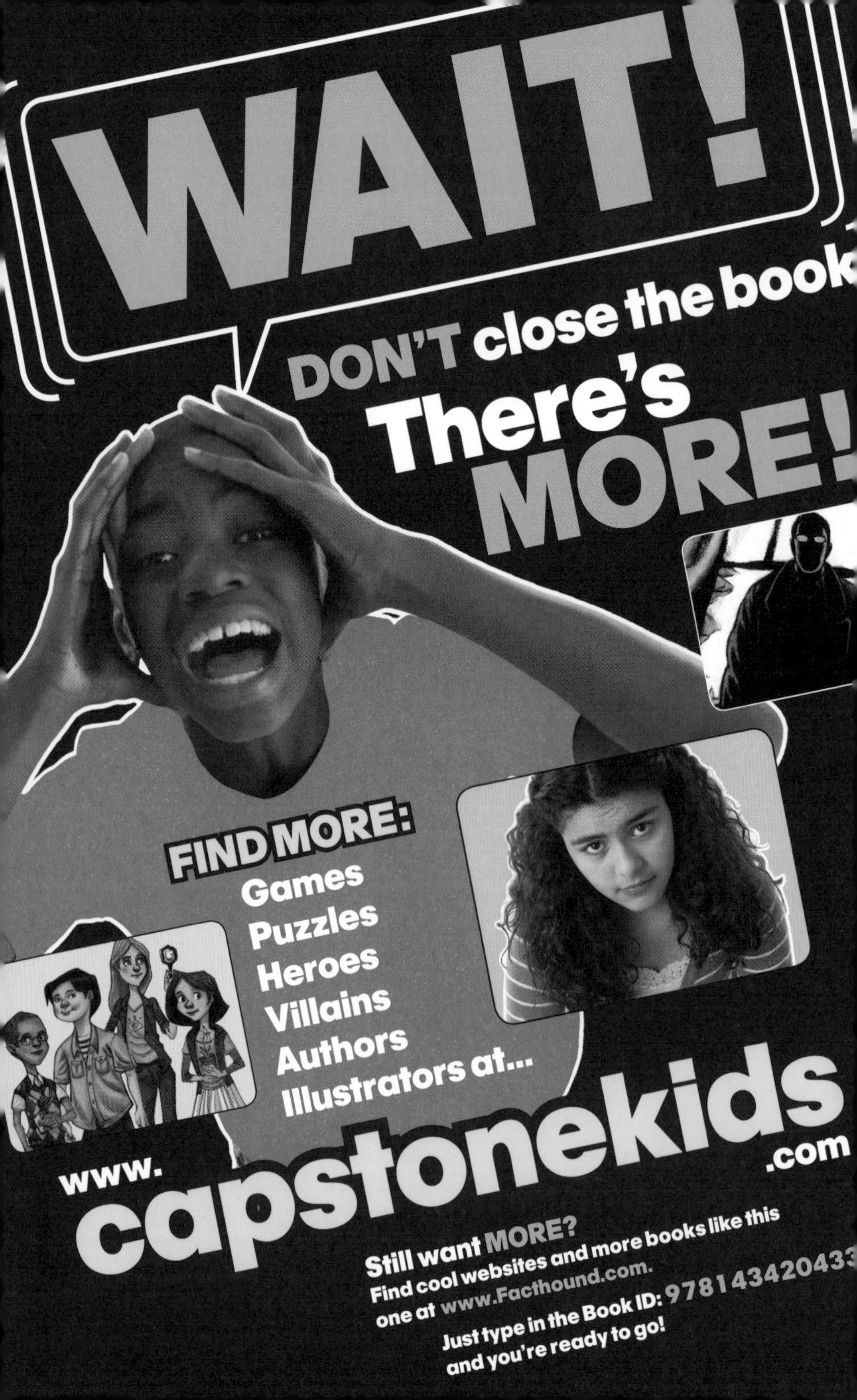
WAIT!
DON'T close the book
There's MORE!
FIND MORE:
Games
Puzzles
Heroes
Villains
Authors
Illustrators at...
www.capstonekids.com
Still want MORE?
Find cool websites and more books like this one at www.Facthound.com.
Just type in the Book ID: 978143420433
and you're ready to go!

Graphic Flash is published by Stone Arch Books,
A Capstone Imprint
1710 Roe Crest Drive
North Mankato, Minnesota 56003
www.capstonepub.com

Library of Congress Cataloging-in-Publication Data
Gunderson, Jessica.
    Ropes of the Revolution: The Tale of the Boston Tea Party / by J. Gunderson;
illustrated by Brent Schoonover.
    p. cm. — (Graphic Flash)
    ISBN 978-1-4342-0433-2 (library binding)
    ISBN 978-1-4342-0492-9 (paperback)
    1. Graphic novels. I. Schoonover, Brent. II. Title.
PN6727.G777R67 2008
741.5'973—dc22   2007032235

Summary: Sam Adams and the Sons of Liberty are planning a protest on British
taxes. On December 16, 1773, they're going to dump shiploads of British tea into
Boston Harbor. Fifteen-year-old Benjamin and his best friend, Joseph, want a part of
the action! Unfortunately, Benjamin's boss won't let him leave rope-making shop. If
Benjamin can't escape, he'll miss the start of the American Revolution.

Art Director: Heather Kindseth
Graphic Designer: Brann Garvey

Printed in the United States of America in North Mankato, Minnesota.
052018   000563

Ropes of Revolution

The Tale of the Boston Tea Party

by **J. Gunderson**

illustrated by **Brent Schoonover**

Librarian Reviewer
Laurie K. Holland
Media Specialist (National Board Certified), Edina, MN
MA in Elementary Education, Minnesota State University, Mankato

Reading Consultant
Elizabeth Stedem
Educator/Consultant, Colorado Springs, CO
MA in Elementary Education, University of Denver, CO

STONE ARCH BOOKS
Minneapolis   San Diego